"A Boy Named Alice"

By

Gunner A. Bush

DEDICATED TO
THE MEMORY OF
UNCLE DANNY

And all the fools on /r/collapse

"The blackness grew over the city like a blackhole might; some of the buildings downtown made popping noises as they went dark. From the Galt House to the Downs, New Lou restaurants to the Oxmoor mall, a tenebrous tint grew across the entire 502." ~Louisville Courier Journal

"Hello, Louisville, can you hear us? The power might be out, but we still have things to do in your area this weekend!" ~ Ethan S. LeoWeekly June 24th

"Who is the Moon Gang? And Why the Power is Out!" ~ Carolyn B. LeoWeekly June 27th

"The Mayor and Governor are currently working with the President to figure out how to get electricity up and running ASAP!" ~Brian S. Wave 3 News

"Who are Nick Moon and the Moon Gang? We have the exclusive look into the electric group of teenagers who cut the power. Full Story at Noon." ~ Valerie C. WDRB

CHAPTER 1

"Everyone believes they are lucky enough to live during the end of the world."

Alice said it matter of factly, but I couldn't argue with her.

Our conversation could go silent for minutes at a time, but pick up right at the same spot.

"Everyone wants to be alive during the end of the world. It's not just me."

Maybe that wasn't correct, but it felt right when I said it.

Alice gazed at me from her awkward position, her long strawberry blonde hair falling across her pale face. She brushed it back and tipped her head back, allowing me to see the rolling of her Mountain Dew colored eyes before her head disappeared back into her side of our shared bedroom.

Our house is so small it hurts. Listed as a two bedroom, Alice and I share the second bedroom, an attic with drywall divided by a clothes rack mom got from a yard sale and a makeshift wall here before we moved in. The entrepreneurial semantics of the landlord didn't end with the listing of two bedrooms; the dead end street we lived on was listed as a cul-de-sac.

It's a dead end house on a dead end street that hosts our dead end dreams.

Alice and I shared a womb, and this room wasn't much bigger.

Alice was plotting her outfit for school the next day, and I was doom scrolling; our nightly rituals.

Alice hated when I compressed the worst news into headlines. My phone contained a plethora of doomsday notes; each one unique with some end of the world scenario.

I flip through it trying to find the saved memo note so I can inform Alice of the incoming apocalypse.

"You do know about a Blue Ocean Event, right?" I asked.

She's listening, but ignoring me. Her favorite.

"A Blue Ocean Event or BOE is when the Arctic Ocean changes from being covered in ice year-round and reflecting most of the sunlight that impacts it back into space to being mostly ice-free blue water for a period of time during the warm season (May till October), which will cause it to absorb most of the sunlight that impacts it."

I pause to ponder what I've just read. It's a lot to take in.

"That doesn't sound as severe as it really is, though. I thought I saved something better."

"What happened to the flu in Asia?" She asked, but I was onto something else.

I begin to search through my notes for a more terrifying outlook about a BOE, Alice breaks her silence.

"You're an Alarmist, Nick. You're always prophesying calamities."

Alice was right, again. She usually is, but she always is when diagnosing me.

I don't respond; I'm searching my notes for more information on the BOE and its imminent destruction of the planet.

I remove the navy blanket that itches my forearms and sit up to read what I've just found.

"Here look, okay, I found it. 'If all the ice covering Antarctica, Greenland, and the mountain glaciers around the world were to melt, sea level would rise about 70 meters (230 feet). The ocean would cover all the coastal cities. And land area would shrink significantly. But many cities, such as Denver, would survive."

I paused again.

"We need to move to Colorado."

I was only 17 so you might be wondering why in the fuck I do this to myself?

There's a simple answer, and a long one.

I create anxieties to remain depressed about the future.

The longer response may be necessary since, even as a 17-year-old, I am aware that death is a fact of life. Death wasn't some distant life event that happened to other people; I see my own approaching fifty-seven times each hour. Knowing this, I feel compelled to seek out a mass event where we may all pass away together out of fear of dying alone.

My ADHD leads me into another one of my old phone notes.

"Oh shit, look at what I wrote about Steve Jobs right after this part about the Blue Ocean Event, 'Steve Jobs died from pancreatic cancer that might have been linked back to his all-carrot diet. At one time, Jobs ate so many carrots his skin tinted towards orange.'"

My navy blanket is on the ground, and I am trying to speak with a sense of urgency that might be palpable to Alice.

"Think about that, Alice, a multi-billionaire and guy who changed the world, was trying to eat healthy, and ended up killing himself."

"Was that a medical diagnosis or something you made up?"

"It's facts. He died from pancreatic cancer."

"Yeah, but was the reason really from his carrot diet?"

Alice could always see through the blanks in my notes.

The words that weren't written were left out on purpose.

Now I didn't respond.

I closed my notes, and went back to doom scrolling; burning away my phone's battery while staring into the abyss of the internet. I'd read about death, a hurricane that swept through and made headlines because it killed 159 and 11 were children younger than me, or I'd scour the dark web videos of ISIS propaganda as they cut off the necks of journalists from the west, and then I'd skip past it as if flipping channels; The goriest videos didn't bother me. I'd become desensitized to anything; everything actually.

It was the purple cow effect of gore and doom.

"You need to get to bed; mom gave me some Robitussin; why don't you drink it?'

"I'm not sick."

"You've been coughing, and it will help you go to sleep."

"I don't have school tomorrow."

Alice knew I didn't have school tomorrow. She did, but I was suspended.

"I don't want to sleep yet; you go to bed."

I shifted it back to her.

Alice tossed the packaged bottle over and it landed on my bed.

"I heard if you drink enough of it you can trip."

I picked up the white and green box.

"Trip? Trip how?"

Alice didn't respond, but Uncle Google was my best friend: "Effects can range from a mild "buzz" to an "out-of-body" feeling to hallucinations, paranoia, and aggression. They can last 30 minutes to 6 hours after you take the drug."

"Six hours? That sounds like bullshit."

"I guess I can try it," I blurted out loud enough for Mom to hear me, but Alice still wasn't responding.

"The child safety on this shit is impossible, but it is just freaking wasted plastic!"

When it finally cracked, I opened the bottle and gave it a sniff.

"Yuck! It stinks like…medicine."

I took a slow drink, realized it wasn't that bad, and chugged half the bottle.

"Dextromethorphan."

The word rolled off my tongue; the liquid rolled down my throat.

Alice could hear me, "Grape. It doesn't taste as bad as I remember."

"Dextro-meth-orphan."

I finished the bottle.

"If it was discovered today, it would be a banned substance."

I made that up, but I said while staring at my phone.

"Sugar would be banned too!" Alice said, her voice muffled just enough for me to know she was facing the wall and seconds away from dreamland.

"Yeah, and coffee, Miss Starbucks."

Alice and I sharing a room wasn't very PC; sharing a womb was fine, but male and female teenage siblings sharing a bedroom is frowned upon in society. That wasn't the biggest issue with our living quarters. We didn't have a door.

Mom could walk up the stairs anytime she wanted without knocking; privacy isn't big on her agenda, anyway.

"This shit leaves a foul taste."

"Dextromethorphan."

I pucker my lips to say it, "DexTRO-meth-O-rphan. Orphan. Dextro-Or-Fan."

"First of all, Alice, this is non-drowsy so it will not help me sleep, and second of all, besides the bad taste so third of all, this shit does not, I repeat, does not, give you a buzz. Give me a buzz? Give you a buzz? Whatever."

"Probably going to deep fry my liver though, or my kidneys, whichever."

Alice was asleep, and my envy grew for her ability to put a cheek to a pillow and sleep within seven minutes.

"Luck be the lady to sleep," I sang out as Frankie might if that's how the song went, and I bounced back into my phone.

"This stuff doesn't taste that bad. It's not good, really, but not bad."

I said it loud so Alice might wake up and know I was upset because I had swallowed the whole bottle.

Alice wasn't responding. Her clothes were picked out, and she was inches away from sleeping. She was actively trying to be a productive member of society.

I sipped the whole bottle until it was gone, but nothing happened. A genie didn't jump out once I hit the bottom so I tossed it into the trash can yelling in a whisper, "Kobe!"

"My stomach hurts, and it didn't even make me tired," I snapped at Alice, but she was dreaming.

Back to doom scrolling; the beginning of the end was near, and I needed to find it.

Chapter 2

When I went to the bathroom 45 minutes later to get ready for bed, something had changed. I recognized I had reached the first plateau as I got to my feet. My body reacted quickly to it. It was like going through life while surfing; everything was going well until you lost your balance. Your eyesight becomes hazy as the water rushes by your head, and you're unsure of what to do.

I didn't know.

It was as if my brain went fuzzy. The world was brighter as if I had turned on an HD option by clicking a button. There was a tilt in the room, and a blue tint slowly covered my vision. It was intense, but it was also only the first plateau.

My side of the room became huge as my vision doubled. Then the room shrunk as I moved my head. My inner body felt a soothing sense of calm as if a warm blanket was covering my veins, coating it with happiness.

Walking was a chore, but my thoughts were brilliant. I had replies to my own thoughts. I instantly felt happy and smarter. It was as if I could understand Einstein's theories, and see the tree my desk was made from. Every light had a tracer, even my alarm clock, and the blue tint was now on everything as if I was wearing glasses.

My thoughts either ran away or carried me. I understood physics and nature, but walking was difficult.

As I slowly tiptoed down the stairs, I entered into a dream world. The blue tint was either still there, and I didn't notice it, or I was getting used to it like a bad smell on a stinky person. The self-smelling immunity, or a commonly understood conception of how you cannot smell yourself when you are drunk.

This calming blue wasn't a color, but more of a melancholy tint over my world. It came with other things as well, including the ability to see that my life didn't matter, but at the same time how important my life was.

Anything was super cool to examine. A simple spoon developed into a fascinating object; if I tilted Mom's cup of old coffee, the liquid swirled like an ocean. I was experiencing a separate level of consciousness that was in between the waking world and sleep. Everything was clear to me, but nothing made sense.

I'd found the meaning of life, and my reason for living. But I also understood that my life was meaningless.

Traversing through the multiple plateaus of a dextromethorphan trip, I eventually arrived on our front porch perfectly aligned with the sun rise as Mom pulled her Ford Focus into the driveway. She greeted me with her dashing smile, that popped her left dimple out, and I had to match. She wasn't aware that I had been up all night, and assumed I was just up early for school.

The buzz I once felt was dissipating as I reversed, slowly crossing the plateaus I once climbed.

Unloading the car, she made her way to me and I watched the tiredness grow over her body like it usually does.

"Oh Nickie, are you awake because you have a cold and can't go to sleep?"

"There is a new cold going around China; It is similar to SARS. It's going to have a massive impact on the planet."

"Nickie, you gotta stay off the internet sometimes."

I shrugged.

"Did you try any of the medicine I bought? Robitussin has magical powers."

The nonchalant way she said it made me ponder if she knew I

was high right then.

I didn't respond. An ant was marching across the banister, and I felt a part of his mission to find food for his family.

"I guess when it warms up, the ants will be back," Mom said as smacked the tiny hunter ant into the yard.

As soon as the ant flew to the grass, I started laughing like a little kid. Then, all I could do was picture his world. He was out hunting, smelling something particularly delicious and sweet, when suddenly he was jacked back 20 feet into the yard.

Maybe if people behaved like ants, there wouldn't be a collapse.

I wasn't sure whether I had just spoken that aloud as I looked up.

"What? Nickie, are you okay?"

"Yeah, Mom, I am just happy to see you. It's Friday."

Mum cherished Fridays. She was a week-long worrywart who became a weekend warrior. Despite the fact that I still had to go to school before my weekend began, hers had already begun when her Friday work stint ended.

"Come inside, I will make you french toast."

The trip was fading away, but it had been wonderful, and there was no better way to top off it than Mom's famous french toast.

"Do you want a ride to school?"

She didn't know I was suspended.

I lied, "naw, thanks; Dylan is coming to get me."

"Okay, well I have to run to grandma's; I will see you after school. You sure you don't want a ride?"

"Dylan will be here soon. He just texted me; we are going to review for our English quiz on the way."

Mom kissed my forehead, stood up, and she left the house in one sweeping motion. That's how she moves in the mornings. It was Newton's Law, an object in motion stays in motion, and if she stopped too long, she would fall asleep and end up a product of working nights for so long.

Dylan wasn't coming to get me, I wasn't going to study for my English quiz. I headed back to the attic, and collapsed into the welcoming pillow on my bed.

Chapter 3

The sound of the backdoor closing jolted me awake, and the rain beating against my window kept me awake.

The door was Mom returning home; she would be asleep soon. The rain drops hitting the window softly created a cadence that begged me back to sleep. The sun was hidden, my room was dark, but for some reason I couldn't go back to sleep.

I waited until the house was quiet again before leaving my bed. Mom was sleeping, so I would sneak out and return when school was over.

As I grabbed my backpack, the note from Mr. Adams fell to the ground.

The big bold letters on top stood out like a fox in a henhouse.

"Sleeping in Class."

Mr. Adams read the three words with a tone of disdain as if I had screwed his dog when he wrote them.

Even insomniacs get their sleep at some point. My insomnia created from my nightly paranoia of doom scrolling and preparing for global thermonuclear war created a feedback loop which led to me sleeping in class.

I'm sorry but not sorry because learning about algebra pales in comparison when placed in a juxtaposition with the inevitable fallout approaching.

I didn't need to solve for X; I was preparing for both a mass flood event and a major drought. I stockpiled canned goods under my bed, and stole shotgun bullets from Wally World. Bullets and homebrew would become currency after the collapse. A barter system only needs so many wheat men.

The end was coming, and I was preparing. The end was a truth, and I saw it coming from a different direction nightly. This led to me catching up on rest during class, and my suspension from school.

Repeat and loop.

Mr. Adams didn't recognize me when I entered his office, but like most would-be tyrants, he pretended to know everything.

"Sleeping in class, again, Mr. Moon?"

Yawning wasn't the correct response.

"Are you being serious right now, Moon?"

He left off the mister this time as if I cared.

I didn't care.

I didn't like his haircut, and I was staring at it as he waited for an answer. On top was a hairless, unattractive portion of skin gleaming with paleness like a flashlight in a movie theater, but around his ears was the remains of a younger person, but the remnants of black were now being littered with gray. It was hideous, and an enigma for any man to have this type of haircut style unless it is for a movie role for a character created for the 12-16 year old female audience to hate.

"Mis-ter Moon!"

His voice cut through my thoughts about his ugly haircut.

"Excuse me; Yawning isn't a sign of fatigue, but rather lack of oxygen to the brain."

He hadn't mentioned my yawning, and I shouldn't have either.

"Yes, Mr. Moon, but the lack of oxygen is caused by fatigue."

His words were typical of a male authority figure in charge of teenagers; everything he said was true and should not be questioned.

The manilla folder in front of him contained information about me. The dreaded permanent record of my presence in Jefferson County Schools.

"Your father would be very disappointed in you, son."

His words cut like a knife, but that was exactly why he said them.

I raised my head, rolled my eyes, and tilted my head away from him. I wanted him to understand that he couldn't hurt me with words. A note in my permanent record about my father's death failed to mention that Pops dropped out of high school in the 10th grade to drive a rig.

I wasn't going to fall for his ruse, besides, the apple didn't fall very far.

"You think about what your father would say over the next two days. Have your mother sign this, and I want a note of why you won't sleep in class anymore. Understood?"

I smirked, nodded, and took the piece of paper he was holding.

Mr. Adams had no idea that every signature on file with my mother's signature was my design; that every angle of her cursive was mine. I'd been forging her name since third grade. My suspension would be nothing more than additional time to prepare for the impending collapse.

I stuffed the note into my backpack, quietly opened the door, and exited while closing it softly. The rain had stopped, but the remnants made the air sticky and gross.

Now, I was thanking Mr. Adams. If it wasn't for him, I might not have ever been introduced to Dextromethorphan.

CHAPTER 4

Buying the bottle of Robitussin felt illicit. I was new to the game, and faked a cough as the teller rang me out.

"Sick," I muttered as she told me the total.

"It's going around," she responded, but she didn't care.

I made my way home, walking over evaporating puddles as the sun beat down on the pavement.

Mom was still sleeping, so I crept in quietly, but Alice was upstairs listening to punk music.

"What's that?" Alice asked me as soon as I made my way up the stairs.

I replied, "Nothing," and threw the bag onto the chair next to my bed.

"It's not nothing. What is it?"

She poked her nose in the bag. I couldn't lie.

"I bought a bottle in case Mom wonders why the bottle she bought is gone."

"You drank the whole thing?"

"What? No, yes, no. "

"You're going to drink that bottle too?"

Alice could read and feel me like braille to Hellen Keller.

"No."

I was lying, and I didn't have a chance.

She continued, "That stuff cannot be good for your liver," but then she went back to her side.

I sat down, glancing at my phone. I didn't have any notifications, but I pretended to be engaged with something.

"Was it really that good?"

I didn't respond.

"It was, wasn't it?"

Silence. I was hitting her with her own treatment.

"Don't get addicted to drinking that shit; it cannot be good for your liver and kidneys."

I couldn't keep up the silence; I didn't have the passive aggressive strength she had.

"Where are you going tonight?" I asked her in an attempt to switch the convo.

"I don't know. I don't feel like doing much. "

I was still lying; I knew exactly what I was doing as soon as she left.

"Nerd."

"Yeah, well, sorry I don't suffer from FOMO."

She snapped, "I don't have FOMO!"

Our moods were clashing, but she didn't want to bicker. She was already dressed and down the stairs before I could speak another word.

As soon as she left, I ripped open the box like it owed me money and twisted the cap off like a drunk. I drank the whole thing, and it was gross. The medical after-taste was vomit-cringing disgusting.

And then I waited and waited, and waited, and waited, but nothing happened.

Fifteen minutes turned into an hour and fifteen minutes and all I felt was sick to my stomach. The intestines can only handle so much cough medicine, and I was at a breaking point. Nausea and vertigo crept in, so I dashed to the porcelain god, hovered over it, and nothing happened. I walked back to my bed and sat down, a small trashcan next to me, ready to catch my stomach.

When I awoke several hours later, the house was still quiet, but a breeze was blowing outside. My alarm clock read 9:52, but I couldn't make up my mind whether it was am or pm.

Mom had texted me to say she wouldn't be home, but she had prepared her famous meal, which was in the fridge. My stomach grumbled, so I went downstairs and microwaved the ribs and mac and cheese from Ruby Tuesday's.

Socks with feet inside them were wiggling around on the end of the couch, and this would alarm most people. I knew it was Dylan. He had recognizable feet.

Dylan was my best friend, but I believe he had a stronger bond with Mom and Alice. He didn't have a key to get in because he didn't need one. Our front door was never locked. When we lived in Clarksville, robbers broke through the window and stole everything. We had to repurchase everything as well as pay for a new window.

So we didn't lock the door. Alice and I were latchkey kids without the latchkey. Dylan slept better at our house than he did his. His parents were divorced but lived together because they were weird as shit.

I ate Mom's special ribs that she brought home in a doggie bag, and then I tossed my napkin high into the air and onto Dylan's face. He was sleeping on his back like a vampire, with his hands crossed on his chest.

"Dude, get this off of me, you freaking dingleberry!"

Dylan loved calling people "dingleberry."

He sat up and hunched over to warm his arms.

"How was vacation?"

He got up and headed into the kitchen to find one of Mom's Cokes.

"I slept. It was blah. "

He found the soda, and popped it open.

"Do you know what Dextromethorphan is?"

"Dextro meth a what?"

"It's an ingredient in cough syrup."

"Like codeine syrup that the rappers talk about?"

"Naw, well, at least I don't think so."

"No."

"It's in Robitussin."

"Oh, the cough syrup?"

"Yeah."

"It's over the counter? Is it like yellow dye number five?"

"I don't know; what is that?"

"It's an ingredient in Mellow Yellow that makes your penis shrink. Doctors told me I should drink it or I will never find a human that will be able to take me."

He turned his fingers and waved them over an imaginary gigantic penis.

"That's dumb."

"Are you talking about robo-tripping?"

"Robo-tripping?"

"Yeah, my cousin in Evansville used to do it, or perhaps he still does. You drink a whole bottle of Robitussin, or take like twenty pills at a time, and it gets you high. "

"Maybe."

"I always thought it was like smoking banana peels."

"What do you mean?" I asked.

"I don't know. I heard back in eighth grade that if you smoked dried banana peels, you can get just as high as smoking marijuana. "

Dylan was full of worthless information that could become valuable at any time.

"That sounds like bullshit."

"Exactly, and that is why I never tried either one."

"What if it does work?"

"Then go ahead and find a monkey cage, gather all the peels, and smoke them. I don't like smoking anything."

"No, not that; I mean the Robitussin."

"Drinking that much would probably kill your liver."

"How? That isn't that much liquid."

"The aspirin, or whatever in it."

"Acetaminophen?"

"Yeah, you can die if you take too much of that shit."

"That shit isn't in Robitussin."

"How do you know?"

"I checked."

"You checked? Did you try this?"

I smiled and nodded, but held back from verbally answering.

"Are you serious?"

"Yep, last night. Alice gave me some, and, uh, she's the one who told me. "

"What? Did Alice do it too?"

"Naw."

He chugged the can.

"Don't drink all Mom's cokes, okay?"

"Is Alice going to be around tonight?"

His eyebrows lifted up when he said it like a child lying; Dylan was always into Alice more than me.

"I don't know."

His coke was done, and he sat back down on the couch.

"I was out there, Dylan. It was like living in a dream. My body had a euphoria about it, and everything was new and fresh."

"Really?"

I had his attention now; his thoughts of my sister disappeared with his interest in my trip.

"Now I'm questioning whether it was a real thing though, because maybe it was a placebo effect."

He scrunched his head, and pulled his face back.

"No, I don't know Dylan; I bought a bigger bottle tonight, and chugged it right after school, but nothing happened."

"I don't think you can trip on back to back days like that; My cousin used to say that about LSD, and he was following Tool around for a bit."

"Really?"

"Yeah, why don't you ask Dr. Google?'

So I did. I cranked robotripping on back to back nights into the search engine, and I discovered the truth. The harsh reality was that human brains are only so primitive. We cannot experience a mind-opening event such as tripping on dextromethorphan every day. Our brain needs to build up serotonin, and create awesomeness before releasing it.

"Damn, so it says it is best to only try it once a week at the most, and once a month is even better," I read to Dylan, who was now flipping through the Direct TV channels.

"Yeah, so you gotta plan it out, and trip like once a week or once every two weeks."

His response was casual, but only because he'd never been there before; if he'd experienced the dreamland, he'd want to go back.

"I need that shit every day like it's fucking air, dude. I cannot plan it out and do one trip a week. I've been there, and I want to go back!"

I was being dramatic, playing it up, but Dylan still didn't care. He had to experience it.

I was elated that this was the case too, because I was fearful I'd never get back.

"I can wait a week, so next Thursday night, and I want you to do it with me, okay?"

"What? Me? No, dude, I can't. Thursdays are bad for me. We got school, I can't. "

"Isn't Friday a snow day or something?"

"Yeah, it's a make up, but I can't, Nick, seriously. I mean -."

He hung his words out to dry like clothes, and Dylan was a man of many words. He wanted to try it.

"It's fucking amazing."

"Really?" His one word question was all I needed to confirm he wanted to try.

"Thursday. You are in, and it is a date!"

His silence was his confirmation.

Alice broke in before I had to go into a full on sales pitch.

She was wearing a fake Burberry raincoat and boots, but was dry as sand.

"Is it raining?" Dylan questioned.

"Not yet."

"Next Thursday, Dylan and I are drinking Robitussin and tripping, and you need to be here."

"What? Why? So I can babysit you two? "

"I guess."

"Seriously, Nick?"

She took off her raincoat, pulling it off and exposing her bare stomach. She was pale but fit. Dylan watched like a hawk does a baby bunny.

I rolled my eyes, "I am going to jump in the shower; I feel dirty."

"Is it that time of the month already?" Alice joked, and she sat down next to Dylan on the couch.

I responded to deflect her joke, "Frank Sinatra would take seven showers a day sometimes.

She sat next to him with their legs touching, and I saw Dylan's hand gliding across her leg.

"Okay," Dylan said, grabbing the old Rolling Stone magazine from the coffee table. Mom kept it as a relic of the 90s or something. Prince was on the cover.

"You didn't go to Graber's party?" Alice asked Dylan, but I left as he answered.

"No, I heard the cops were coming, and Derrick was throwing people out."

I was standing in front of the steamy mirror, banging my head repeatedly, trying to remove water from my ear when the silence from the other room struck me as odd. Straining my ears to carefully hear something, all I heard was a smacking sound. At first, my body was so discombobulated from the hot shower that I didn't put one and two together. The sound was lips smacking in between light moans.

Luckily, before I opened the bathroom door, I realized what it was, and I didn't jerk the door open like I usually do. The bathroom door has a creak that will wake the dead, but I didn't tug on the door to alarm them. I pulled it open about a foot and slithered through.

I crept into the living room like a hitman, and I saw it with my own eyes. My best friend and sister were making out. It was beyond that stage, and headed for worse actually. If I was playing baseball, they were heading towards third. They both had their shirts off, and Dylan hovered over her, dropping his pants.

I was mortified. More shocked than mortified, but my head shook hard and I pinched myself. Since they were 18, it was two consenting adults, but it was also my best friend and my sister.

It's not that I have some 'roll tide' love for my sister, but I didn't want her to be having sex. I didn't appreciate the sneakiness either. I had only been in the shower for ten minutes, and they were going at it like jackrabbits.

But it wasn't just the sneakiness, it was also the fact that it was my best friend and my sister. We were close as brothers since we'd met, so I did what any reasonable brother might do, and I screamed like a female.

"Hey! Stop! "

And they did too. Most everybody would have since I screamed like a young lady being hit by a car.

Dylan rushed for his jeans, and Alice bounced upstairs like she had coals on the bottom of her feet.

"What the hell, man?" I begged.

"What the hell, you man?" Dylan replied. He was trying to pull his pants up, but his foot got stuck, and he fell forward onto the couch.

"I stopped, Jesus, Alice."

"Alice?" I questioned. I didn't want him to blame her for me stopping it, but I was also mad at her.

"You want us to stop? Fine! We will stop. We stopped. I am

fucking leaving! "

His face was red, full of embarrassment, and he spit when he cussed.

I didn't respond; I was naked too. My towel fell at some point.

He turned to button his pants and looked at me before he opened the door. His eyes were red with a chance of tears popping out of the corners.

Empathy kicked me in the face; he obviously liked Alice.

"Look, Dylan, I didn't know, shit, if you want to fuck Alice, then fuck Alice, okay?"

"Fuck Alice?" He snapped back as if I was an idiot.

"Fuck you and your Alice!"

I scrambled to find my towel.

"It's okay, Dylan, you don't have to leave. You want to just talk to Alice?"

"No, dude, I don't want to talk to Alice. It is fine. I am leaving."

The rain was ticking against the house, and the wind was blowing, but he left anyway.

I sat down on the couch, and before I could even comprehend what had just happened, Alice slammed something upstairs. She was pissed. She was stomping around, so I heard every single step, and then she slammed something else.

"What the fuck," I whispered to myself, but I wanted Alice to hear me too.

I couldn't avoid the encounter forever, so I slowly stood up, wrapped the towel around myself, and made my way upstairs.

CHAPTER 5

The week crawled by so slowly that it felt like Thursday would never arrive. Dylan didn't come over all week, but I sat next to him every day in class. We barely spoke.

I didn't bring it up to Alice either. It was her choice, but I didn't really see her a lot either.

Anxiety ran through my body on Wednesday night, and after six days of googling more information about the plateaus and the do's and don'ts of a robotrip, I decided to get some exercise.

A storm was coming in from the south, which isn't unusual but usually means it will be a thunderstorm. That's the best time in the world for me; when the air is full of humidity but the breeze keeps you cool. The trees were swaying like rock concert fans. It's calm before the storm, but it's never calm.

I walked up the boulevard wearing my hoodie, but it wasn't cold. It was helping me to sweat out any toxins, and I was having a good time on my walk when a Blazer with rims and tint rolled by a few times. It had extra bright lights and music bumping out of the back.

Until I turned at St. Peter's church to go home, I didn't give it any thought. Small sprinkles of rain were informing me every few seconds that it was about to start pouring.

The Blazer turned down the main road as I cut through the park.

Shit. The Blazer's lights hit me.

I accelerated my speed when I heard someone call my name, since I assumed it was some riff raff looking for trouble.

"Ain't you Nick Moon?"

Glancing over my shoulder, I couldn't make out who it was, so I turned my whole body.

The Blazer was diagonal to me; I squinted and saw it was Joey Fryar. Joey was in my class, but more of a jock and someone I never associated with, ever.

I was surprised he knew my name.

Our one encounter was a freshman year when we were both assigned the same locker. I sat by him multiple times and had him in several classes, but we never spoke. He was a jock and popular and headed to a frat somewhere at a state college, and I was heading towards dropping out.

I turned around and kept walking away while shouting, "No."

The rain was about to start, and I didn't want to bother with whatever Joe Fryar had up his sleeve.

The temptation was there though, because Joey wasn't the prom king, but he was on the prom row, popular and all that jazz.

I quickened my pace and finally took a breath when I could no longer hear him.

Somehow, the rain held off, and the wind calmed, so when I approached my house and saw the lights on, meaning Mom was awake, I took a detour. I didn't want to see her before she went to work. She would ask a hundred and one questions, and I didn't want to deal with it.

Detouring through the alley, I walked towards Bloom Elementary.

The street lights were on, but the motion from the playground took a while to register; as I got closer, I saw two people near the swings. I took the long route and moved in the direction of the walking track because I didn't want any trouble. They would mind their own business, I reasoned, and I would mind mine.

I heard the female voice yelling. "Stop it, hey, stop it!"

I rushed over without even pausing.

"No, I like it rough. Don't stop."

I slowed my roll a bit because there were mixed signals. I didn't want to be a hero, but I had to look up and see what was going on. As my vision focused on the couple, the male figure grabbed her by the wrist.

"Yo, hey, you. What are you doing?"

It was loud and boisterous, with an extra deep voice to sound intimidating.

It was Joey Fryar, but that wasn't what surprised me. The thunderbolt was the female figure. It was Alice.

"Alice, what the?"

Being mad at Alice wasn't right because it was Joey twisting her arm back.

"Why are you holding her arm like that?"

I reached for his arm to remove it from her wrist, but I couldn't. Joey was quick, and he dropped her wrists and held mine so fast I didn't even see it.

"You were into it a minute ago, Alice. I thought you liked it rough. "

He said Alice, but he stared at me before ripping his arm off of my wrist.

"Fuck off, Joe Fryar," I said his full names in hopes to wake him up out of his steroid induced rage.

The urge to hit him grew. Somehow, I held it back.

"Why don't you stop being a bully," I quipped, clutching my wrist.

"A bully? A minute ago you were trying to give me top, and now you are calling me a bully. "

"Yeah, that is what I wanted to do; come on, Alice, let's go."

I helped Alice up. Her knees were cut from when she fell, and she was wearing a dismal face.

"You better leave us alone, or I will tell everyone what happened!"

Spit flew out with the words. My anger was full tilt, and I made sure to stare at Joey so Alice would know I wasn't upset with her.

Shaking his head, he began to walk towards his Blazer, "You, Alice, whatever, you can go fuck off!"

He was the typical bad guy in the movie, thinking he could do whatever he wanted, especially with the ladies, and never have to pay for the consequences of his actions. It was typical white privilege bullshit that guys like Joey constantly deny even exists.

Joey drove away, squealing his tires like a child, and I threw my arm around Alice's shoulder as we walked home. Neither of us said a word. I didn't know what to say, so I squeezed her shoulder tight as we strolled. I needed her to know I was on her team, despite her being a slut.

The rain hit as soon as we reached our street. It wasn't brisk,but it was slowly picking up as we arrived. Mom was backing up, leaving for work, as we arrived, and she rolled down her window.

"Y'all need to get inside! I thought you were asleep!"

"We are going, we are going!"

"Go!"

"Alice couldn't sleep, so we went on a walk," I lied, but we both picked up our pace to get inside.

"Okay, I love you, Nick."

"I love you too, Mom!"

The silence didn't cease. Alice took a shower and came upstairs with a towel on, and then she stared out the window as the raindrops fell. The hypnotic sound of the rain beating on our roof was beautiful. Being in the attic sure had its advantages.

I spoke softly, but in a childlike tone, "Goodnight, Alice."

"Night, Nick."

She didn't turn her head.

For the first time in years, I fell asleep before her.

CHAPTER 6

School on Thursday crept by slower than an old lady exiting a gas station bathroom. The clock wouldn't move, and the teachers preached in slow motion. It was beyond agony. When the misery finally ended, I purposefully ran into Dylan as he walked out the side door to freedom.

"You still coming by tonight?"

His movement halted, but he didn't immediately turn to face me.

"Alice wants you to come over." I added, as if pity was my only option.

Before responding, Dylan turned to face me and narrowed his brown eyes, "I planned on it."

"Great. I already bought the stuff."

"Cool. What time?"

"Mom leaves around nine so?"

"I will be there, but after that. I gotta wait until Mom goes to sleep."

We didn't say anything else. He went to his step-dad's truck, and I headed home.

When Joe's Blazer passed while I was making my way home, my heart skipped a beat. I did everything in my power to hide the rush of stomach to chest. As he turned around, I noticed my reflection in the mirror-tinted glass.

After continuing down the alley, I once more came across the Blazer now on my street; it was likely leaving the dead end and searching for Alice.

A folded card with a yellow flower protruding from it sat on the welcome mat beside the front entrance.

Alice,

Sorry about last night, and listen, I really mean that. I thought we were playing like that with wrestling or whatever, and I guess I took it too far. I hope we can hang again sometime, but I understand if you don't want to.

You have my number, and I will always respond to your texts.

Oh, and if you don't want to hang, I guess thanks for not telling anybody about us, and I promise you, I will never tell a soul.

Joey

The note was crinkled and tossed before I finished reading his name.

What a douchebag! Alice wasn't getting the note.

I burned the message in the firepit while clenching my fists in fury. One of those "be careful what you wish for" conundrums of a rock and hard place; I wanted Alice to date anyone but Dylan, but now, I'd give anything for her to go back to Dylan.

Mom still had a sock on her doorknob when I entered, so I knew she was dozing off at the time. That served as the signal in our home, where it's crucial to maintain silence while the sock is on the doorknob because one parent of a one-parent family works nights. Mom absolutely needed to sleep. Out of the recycling, I took an empty Coke can and filled it with water. I inserted the yellow flower's stem inside it and placed it on the counter for Mom. She would awaken and discover it.

As I made my way upstairs, a choir started to chant to me; the three Robitussin bottles under my bed yearned to be opened and consumed.

"Please, open us, let's go!"

"Nick, it's Thursday. Thursday is the day you drink us!"

It was impossible to ignore, and nothing distracted me.

I had been reading about dextromethorphan all week in chat rooms, subreddits, secret forums, and anywhere else I could find it. I went from being a complete novice to an expert who knew everything there was to know about the drug in just seven days.

The looping of my frontal lobe was only on tripping so I felt pulled to drink a bottle.

By the time Mom got up to leave for work, I was salivating at the mouth to drink the stuff.While Mom got ready, I held off and pretended to be asleep while keeping my lights off. I wanted to talk to her, but I also wanted her to believe that I was asleep at 10 o'clock like a nice, decent kid would.

When I finally worked up the guts to go say hello to her, she had left. She slammed the front door shut as soon as I reached the last step. She had put a sticky note on the drink can with the flower inside even though she had departed.

Thanks for the flower, Nick, have a great night.

Alice walked in less than five minutes later wearing clothes a father would despise his daughter wearing, but we didn't have a father so Alice dealt with her daddy issues in another way.

"What are you wearing?"

You aren't blind; you can see what I'm wearing, she appeared to be saying as her hand and face moved accordingly.

And I could. She wore a red crop top with her pale abs showing, a black miniskirt designed for a small circus monkey, and black knee-high boots.

She didn't respond and looked at herself in the mirror by the door so I asked again.

"What are you, my dad?"

"No, Alice, is that what this is about? Dad?"

"Dad? What are you talking about, Nick?"

She spoke with a lot of snark. I saw her open the refrigerator and bend down to retrieve something while wearing thong panties.

"Jesus, Alice, first Dylan, and then Joe Fryar of people, and tell me, who was it tonight?"

She didn't say anything, but her expression spoke volumes. Although I was the one who had saved her from Joe, she was disgusted with me for meddling in her life.

"We're not discussing this," She replied and sipped on some of Mom's wine while eating cold mac and cheese.

Although I was heated with agitation, I was unsure of what to say or do. What could I do if she decided to meet up with Joe Fryar or Dylan because it was her life?

"Are we still doing that thing tonight?" She asked me with her mouth full of cheesy noodles.

"That thing?" I inquired.

She gave me a nod as if I should understand what she was saying. Although I did, I didn't want her to believe I did.

She swallowed and snapped, that thing.

I guess we are, she said as she threw the empty mac and cheese container in the garbage.

We didn't talk until Dylan knocked and let himself into the house about five minutes later.

Turning to Dylan, she questioned, "What's up with the drum?"

"Bongo drums."

"Yeah, but why?"

"So I read while you are tripping, well, on LSD or mushrooms, that playing music can really make sure you are in a happy place. I can't play any instrument, but anyone can play bongo drums, right?"

"I don't think I can," I added, and I wanted to pick on myself.

"I don't have any timing or rhythm."

Dylan smiled.

That's what I wanted.

We went upstairs and gagged our way through drinking a bottle each of the purple stuff. Alice almost didn't drink all of hers because she didn't like the medical taste. Alice got through it by holding her nose.

"I don't feel anything," Dylan said seven minutes later.

"Yeah it takes a long time for it to kick in; last week, it took over an hour and I read about cases taking even longer."

Dylan nodded, and he began to show me how he also didn't have any rhythm as he banged on his drums.

Alice and created a small fire in the backyard as Dylan tried to find a cadence. Playing the bongo drums without rhythm is like running without legs. The interest waned. Alice was decent at the drums, but she said her hand went numb so we gave up on that idea.

The fact that Dylan brought drums, and his reasoning for bringing them, meant he had been on google just as much as me. He was reading different blogs because his goal was to have a happy, safe trip with laughter and bongo drums, and I wanted to hit the furthest plateau and possibly learn the meaning to life.

I desired a safe haven and not just for me but for us. Life is better with friends, and I had two of the best, so I couldn't let it bother me that they were romantically involved behind my back. I knew about it now, and I had to make sure they knew it was A-okay.

It was all a grand vibe, and I was smiling ear to ear before the trip arrived. It hit perfectly, but the company was even better.

CHAPTER 7

Thursday nights at the Moon house on the dead end street turned into a thing. We didn't intend it to happen, but that's how it usually happens. And by thing, I mean, a party of high school teenagers without being a high school party.

Our house was the quintessential location for a massive party. It was on a dead end street with a wooded area to the south, and 81 year old Mrs. Hartke owned the house to the north; she was living in assisted living after breaking her hip. Her son came by once a week to check the mail and cut the grass, and that was never after 10 pm on a Thursday.

Mom's being gone was the perfect situation too.

So it grew from Nick and Dylan and me to a few more people, including Amber, who was one of Alice's only girlfriends in the entire school. The viciousness of the other girls in high school created their alliance.

Having one good girlfriend to walk among the wolves of other females is priceless, Alice told me.

Amber's twin brother, Jackson, didn't go to school with us; he'd dropped out to work at a garage. That was Amber's goal too, but she was getting her piece of paper that said diploma first. Amber was rough around the edges and needed a caution sign for some folks. She didn't care about the boys either.

Eric "Goomba" Williford was another addition; he'd been in classes with me since freshman year. Gomba was short, unathletic, and unapologetic about it. He wore glasses that hung low over his acne filled cheeks, and he fashioned lamb chop sideburns. He was a character.

Goomba's nickname came from his love of the Super Mario games on Nintendo; he wore Mario and Luigi shirts to school, but he also wore a hat with a Goomba on it when he was allowed. Most of the teachers put up with it because he was fully grown at 5'3 and overweight.

Alice and I didn't care about his imperfections, though. Jesus was perfect and they killed him, so Goomba was okay to hang with us on Thursdays. He was also well read and added a lot of interesting perspectives to our conversation.

Goomba was already enrolled in and taking community college courses and was a wiz when it came to computers. His real voice was high pitched, but he dropped it on Thursday nights. He also understood why I doom scrolled.

"The system of capitalism is corrupt as fuck. It was invented in the 16th century, and what followed was mass genocide, slavery, and some of the worst parts of recorded history. "

He smoked clove cigarettes, and despite his not caring, he was a prime example of why high school is a sham. He wasn't popular, and wouldn't be popular in any school in America, but he was smart, witty, edgy, and a conversationalist who understood how the puppet show worked.

"I'm only taking classes at JCC because it is free. I could have gone to UK or U of L, but I would have had to pay. My family cannot afford to pay, so what is my only other option? I gotta take out student loans and owe on those for the next 30 years. That is modern day slavery!"

Goomba wasn't alone. All of us saw older cousins or siblings take out loans for the "college education" that is required to live in America, and now they were all in debt. They went to dead end jobs and sent off their resumes and applications when they were supposed to be working.

Student loans are the modern-day equivalent of slavery.

The six of us spent every Thursday for a month together. We brought facts about how the system was broken, but more importantly, we all knew the world was ending. All six of us agreed that a collapse was incoming, and we all sort of agreed that it was due.

"The baby boomers scorched the earth; Especially here in America! They were the kids of the parents who killed the Nazi's, so they thought nothing they did could be wrong. They were self-righteous and full of greed."

He was monkey-fucking a clove off of one of Dylan's Reds and killing it. He puffed his clove hard, blew out the smoke, and continued, "Freaking Gordon Gekko! He turned into a hero with his greed, and it is good bullshit. Gekko was supposed to be the villain! Greed isn't good, greed is terrible. The greed of money is the root of all evil! That shit is in the bible, right?"

"Yet, in America in the 1980s, the cocaine infused 80s with Reagan and his cheating, the baby boomers decided to fuck it all up! They ran up the debt, never put back into education, yet made a college education essential even though it costs an arm and a leg, and most importantly, they didn't do shit about climate change. The biggest chunk of people kicked the can even though action was needed! Their parents fought fascism and won! These idiots all read Hemingway's losing to fascism in school, and then went home and saw their parents who beat the fascists, and they only turned it into greed! The Boomers accomplished nothing! They lost in 'Nam, and the moon landing was all done by their parents. The Boomers were in high school or in diapers when Armstrong walked on the moon. They couldn't even keep the space program alive."

"Fuck the Boomers!" Dylan exclaimed, and we all cheered.

"The debt for a college education is a scam; you borrow money from rich people to get an education that will make you more efficient at making rich people money, and in return the rich folks give you a wage which you use to pay them back for going to school. It's a vicious cycle."

"Yeah, fuck the Boomers!"

So we all agreed on almost everything. Six like-minded individuals talking about climate change, and how our grandparents screwed us over.

"I don't have a retirement; I will do like most of you in the climate crisis or from the fallout," Goomba added after our cheers.

As word got out, we couldn't keep it just the six of us.

None of us wanted to expand beyond anything more than just a safe place for everyone who wanted a safe place. We didn't even want it to leak out that the house was empty, and we were having parties, but keeping a house party a secret in high school is impossible.

The leaking started with Joey Fryar, but I don't want to put all the blame on him.

Staying away from Joey after what happened was easy, and I thought it was all over with so when he ran up from behind me, while I was walking home, I was paranoid from the jump.

"Hey, can I talk to you?"

His voice was timid and soft. He was afraid and completely out of his element.

Glancing at him once before turning away, he was like a child confessing to a priest.

"Whatcha wanna talk about, huh? Let me guess, Alice?"

"Yeah, uh, Alice."

"Okay, so?"

"Yeah, I mean, I know you got the note I wrote, and the flower, but look, uh, I would never hurt you or -"

"Hurt me? I know you would never hurt me because I would fucking kill you, but if you ever hurt Alice!"

"Hey, look, okay, that's what I was about to say. Calm down."

"Don't tell me to calm down!" I gritted the words out through my teeth.

"Right, uh, okay, so like even that night at the elementary school, I was just playing rough, like wrestling, it wasn't anything else. If you had said stop, I would have stopped right away. I respect boundaries and the word no. I am not a complete jerk. "

His charm was on full display, and it was working. Guys with good looks, like Joey, learn charm first and foremost. Their innate survival instinct evolved in Ancient Greece.

"Yeah, well, did Alice say no?"

"What? No, of course not, and you know this."

"I will have to ask her."

"What?"

"I didn't stutter."

The misunderstanding of what I said grew on his face.

"I did not stutter," I repeated.

"I respected your boundaries!"

"Yeah, when you threw me and Alice on the ground?"

"No, that was wrong, and look, I am sorry, but everything was going fine, and then…"

"And then I showed up and ruined it?"

"What?"

"You said everything was fine, and then?"

"And then…"

"Right, it was all going fine, and then I showed up, right?"

"No, I didn't say that. You said that. "

"That's what happened, right?"

"Can I talk to Alice?"

He was pitiful. He was wearing a tank top, and his upper arm muscles jiggled with his emotions, and looking at him with his dreamy black hair, handsome face, and cutting blue eyes, I understood why Alice talked to him.

"You must like her because aren't you dating what's her name?"

"Brooke? No, we broke up."

"Then why do you like Alice?"

"You know why."

"Oh, I know why, huh?"

He looked down; his awkwardness was unnerving, and this was an unfamiliar action from anyone on the right side of popularity as a senior.

"You like Alice?"

"Yeah," He perked up.

His puppy-dog excitement befuddled me.

"Why don't you join us on Thursday night at our house; you

know where you left the flower."

"Thursday? Sure, what time?"

"Our Mom leaves around nine, so after that; we can drink wine and 'tussin."

"Tussin?"

"Robo-tripping; have you ever heard of it?"

"I don't know, but I would love to hang out with you and, uh, Alice."

He walked off confused, but I have to admit, I was confused about why he approached me about Alice. It would have been just as easy to text Alice, or even talk to her as she walked home. Perhaps it was some sort of gentleman's code, since Alice didn't have a father. And I rushed him when I thought he was hurting Alice.

Alice was home when I arrived, but she was dressed to go out.

"Guess who I ran into?"

"Who?"

"Are you going somewhere?"

"Maybe."

"Joey Fryar."

"And?"

"And? You know what, let me ask you something. "

"What?"

"Before I showed up when you two were at the playground, did, uh, well," Getting the words out was like pulling teeth.

"What, Nick?"

"Before I showed up, you two were having a good time?"

Her silent response was my answer.

"So I messed it up?"

Again, her silence said everything.

"Damn Alice, I thought you liked Dylan."

"You didn't like it when I liked him either!"

"I didn't know you two were secretly messing around until I walked out of the shower and found out!"

Our voices were climbing.

"You freaking knew; do not act like that!"

It's difficult to remember events when trying to, and yet the ordeal with Joey at the playground, I couldn't piece it together.

Did Joey grab her wrists, or were they just playing?

Alice stormed downstairs, and I sank low while trying to remember.

It was a puzzle in my brain, but the more I thought about it, the more I couldn't remember.

Maybe Joey wasn't grabbing Alice maliciously, and it was merely flirting.

My tail between my legs I bounced downstairs and asked Alice.

"He wasn't hurting me, but when you showed up, well, I didn't know what to do."

The truth is hard to digest sometimes, and it went down like rancid milk mixed with Tabasco sauce.

"Dylan's sister, Chloe, is coming over Thursday too."

"Dylan has a sister?"

"You can meet her on Thursday."

"Okay."

The truth was still digesting, and it was stuck in my esophagus. And I was the one who invited Joey over.

"I invited Aurora to come over too," Alice said nonchalantly.

"Uh, okay."

"And her brother, Cash, might come too."

"Jesus, Alice, did you invite Vice Principal Adams too?"

"No, but should I?"

"Well, didn't you say you wanted to be popular? Now you are. ""

"No, I never said that. Ever."

Alice smiled at me. It was Mom's smile.

Thursday was going to be wild AF.

CHAPTER 8

At the firepit, Dylan and his sister Chloe, Aurora and her brother Cash, Amber and Jackson, and Goomba encircled the firepit as Joey and his sister Wanda showed up. The tension was thick, but Joey recognized it and cut it with his warm blade of likeable personality.

Joey was Mr. Popular, so seeing him arrive without any warning was a shocker. We were the misfits, and unlike most teen movies, we never expected to be interacting with Joey and definitely not Wanda. They were on the other end of the spectrum, so it was peculiar until Joey approached Goomba.

"I like your shirt. Do you ever play any RPGs or any shooter games?"

It was a peace pipe, and Goomba took it. Joey waved at Alice while talking to Goomba, and Wanda sat right next to him.

"Yeah, man, Pokemon counts, right?"

Joey laughed, so I laughed, and Goomba laughed.

The tension dissipated, and we broke into our normal routine. Our safe place was safe again.

Alice cut through the talking to address us, "We want to welcome our new members here tonight, and I hope they know the rules of Moon Gang."

Wanda and Joey made eye contact and shrugged.

"Joey, Wanda, do you know the rules?"

She stood over Joey, representing us as our leader; she was our Joan of Arc, our Wonder Woman, and her role was to lead us on a safe trip. She would guide us through the plateaus brought on by the marvels of modern pharmaceuticals. She was wearing a blue dress with a flower tucked into her long hair at the top; a reminder of Alice in Wonderland.

Thursday nights were our chance for escapism into Wonderland, with Alice leading us. We were the lost boys who found a home, and it became our place to think wishfully.

The fire popped and brightened, and Joey and Wanda wondered what in the hell he had entered. Was it a good place or a bad one? A heaven or a hell? Talking to the unpopular kids isn't that hard when getting laid is on the line. He was staring at us with the fear of a dare, but he didn't know what it was, and his deer in the headlights look wasn't lost on us.

"Oh Wanda, you are so pretty!" Amber gushed over the silence.

"Thank you," Wanda puffed her yellow hair, "What are the rules?"

Alice smiled her devilish smile, "Well, since it is your first night here with the Moon Gang, you must abide by our rules, and that means you've got to drink on

Reflecting light from the fire bounced off Goomba's glasses and right into the palms of Alice as she brandished one unopened bottle of Robitussin in one hand, and a large bottle of Robitussin pills in her other.

Joey bent his head back, "Alice and the Moon Gang, I like that!"

It was time to meet the white rabbit.

"That has to be bad for my stomach," Joey said, rubbing his tight abs through his white collared shirt.

Wanda took the bottle from Alice. Her face was timid and full of fear.

"We've studied the science," I remarked.

I did some research of my own, and let me be the first to say that robo-tripping is a terrible name. Can we come up with something better? "

Wanda didn't wait for an answer. She twisted the cap off, tossed the plastic wrapper into the fire pit, and chugged the bottle as we howled.

Joey grimaced after he drank his, and we continued to howl. Joey joined us in our barbaric chants.

We were young and ready to experience life, and the only way to do that was with substances to alter our reality. When he finished, Joey grimaced, but then he too howled at the half-full moon.

We took in the young night, drinking stolen wine and hot beers, and walking around the empty streets of the Highlands without fear or care. Sitting under the moonlight around the firepit as the still of morning arrived was bliss; even the quiet breaks from conversation were full of talking.

We were young, and growing old felt like something that wouldn't ever happen to us.

CHAPTER 9

And so it was born; the size grew every week, and our backyard became a safe haven for outcasts. All were invited and many came. The requirements were simple, be chill, respect others, and trip. Those were the written rules, but there were also unwritten rules.

Alice was our leader, so she began the meetings which sometimes included, "The first rule of fight club is?"

We'd all laugh and respond, "Don't talk about fight club."

"Welcome to Thursday's with the Moon Gang, and if this is your first night with us, you gotta trip!"

Then she would read something, maybe *Walden* by Thoreau, or lyrics from Zack de La Rocha, or a passage from *The Prince* Machiavelli, but she always read something by Tupac. Tupac Amaru Shakur became our folk hero.

Then we'd howl at the moon, and our night would begin. Even if the moon wasn't visible, we'd still go crazy like it was. We'd announce ourselves as Moonlighters or the Moon Gang; both variations were born out of someone's drunken mouth, "Moonlighting with the Moon Gang," became our rallying cry.

The marketing slogan after our name would have been, "If you accept us, we will accept you." Those were the unwritten rules, and the whole thing was freaking simple. Local pharmacies ran out of Robitussin, so we had to branch over to Indiana to stockpile more. We didn't drink it every week, but we drank enough of it. Some people only drank it their first time, but others drank it every single time.

"No phones allowed!" I collected the tracking devices, and placed them in a shoebox. "It's the glory days, we need to talk and relish in our glory."

"Alice, you should say, the first rule of Gay Fight Club is," Dylan cackled after he said it, but Alice obliged.

We checked into life and out of social media; the moonlight and fire lit the way as we masqueraded with different faces and sparked long discussions mixed with movie quotes. Collectively, we agreed the patriocharchy would soon be deceased, and some believed it was already deceased. Every politician was too old to understand us, and we decided the *only* president that could actually lead the world into the future was likely Seth Rogen. Once we established that he couldn't be President because he wasn't born in the US, we agreed that it should happen even more so.

We loved to bash authorities and the people that be, and we all lied and said we wouldn't end up like them. We were the modern SLC Punks, and we wouldn't conform later; we wanted to stay young forever because growing up was a scam.

The future was bleak, and we began to question why it looked so dim. Our retirement plans wouldn't exist in the future, and it wasn't because the social security would be used up to pay for better paying Senator jobs. No, our future would be filled with war and famine and heat waves brought to you by mega-corporations. We all agreed society would collapse before we even thought about retirement, so why should we sign up to work per hour anywhere? Scientists had been screaming it since the 70s, and now, we would reap because the Boomers didn't sow.

Then we all began to question if we would have done anything, or we would have watched big oil rape the planet. When we agreed we would try, it was us being naive, but we did want to be different.

It was Alice who asked, "can't we do something now?"

It was a simple question, but Alice was right. Shouldn't we try to prevent the incoming collapse? If not us, then who? We couldn't point the finger without looking in the mirror. So the idea rooted and it began to grab ahold of each one of us.

Our weekly meetings consisted of us masquerading as different people inside the Moon Gang as one unit; we were hiding in plain sight under the moonlight, and conversation turned to plans; We were an undefined group of like minded individuals meeting once a week, and our energy grew like wildfire. The ball of moving fire was a youthful movement, progressing forward at a reckless speed. Our purpose was simple, have fun, and our fire was not controlled because we didn't know what we were pushing forward towards. We were just spitballing ideas into the firepit on how to save life on the planet, but didn't have a real agenda or plans. We were just kids barking at the moon.

Well, until Alice decided to change all that.

CHAPTER 10

"Einstein said that all matter has energy. All things have energy. We all have energy, and think about us, right? " I was drunk on cheap wine, but more importantly, I was Tussin, and I was trying to repeat Alice's words.

"Yeah," Auroria said as she nodded, a freshly lit black and mild in her lips; her hair gel straight up on the top, but flat forming sideburns on the side. Her dark eyes were slanted and glazed; her chapped lips puckered when she wasn't talking.

"So what about us, the Moonlighters, right?"

"The Moon Gang Mulligans!" Exel interrupted to add. He was twisted, and his knees were heavy.

"I like that," I replied.

Exel was new to the area, a graduate of some private high school south of Cincinnati full of bigots and daddy's money, but he'd found a new home in our city, and new friends in us. A short man, only 5'5, wore a long, stylish beard, and he hid his receding hairline with a Bearcat hat.

"Brandy came up with that one."

Exel's sister, Brandy, only visited about once a month, but she was lovely. She was a thinker, but she talked about as much as Exel. She was hilarious because she never bit her tongue.

"Brilliant!" I responded.

"So, what is the purpose of all of this?" Brandy asked; Exel was gone. She'd asked on her very first visit, and even before her trip arrived.

"Yes, I would like to know too," Steven, a junior from the all boys Catholic school, added. His sister, Jane, was standing behind him with matching red hair. They both shared pasty skin that never saw the light of day always hidden behind SPF 50 or better.

A ring formed around Alice, and we all waited for an answer.

Yet, for the first time, Alice didn't have one. It was like she could compute some numbers and then tell us all, "The meaning of life is forty-two," or something along those lines. The meaning of our meetings was the meaning of us, and it had to have a purpose, right? We were vain enough to think so at first, but like a zebra in the jaws of a lion, we realized we weren't important.

That's why Alice came up with the Einstein all energy analogy that I repeated to Aurora, who missed the session because of punishment issued by her step-father; she was caught returning to the house early one Friday morning and served a month sentence.

"We should conquer the world," Aurora said, and it was a growing sentiment and repeated slogan that had lost its luster.

"Kings ruled with less," Exel reminded us, but it was another repeated hashtag.

"Conquer the freaking world, huh?"

"In what capacity?" Goomba asked as the hippie Rex strummed an acoustic guitar. Rex was lanky like his arms came from a taller man; it made his guitar playing fantastic.

"That is the big question," I added.

The backyard was full. Glancing around at the different faces and skin colors and people that I now called family, I began to think of an answer.

"What are we doing?"

Alice turned to me, her face informing me she had an answer before she even spoke.

"Let's talk,"she begged, so I followed her.

We walked back towards the back fence that led to the small wooded area behind our house, as Rex reminded the group, "Those who rule let it go to their heads, and then they lose their heads."

Exel snapped, "You should write a song about that."

Rex laughed, and began to sing.

Alice's forehead wrinkled as she began to speak, "We won't be young forever, Nick."

"Yeah, but we are now, so we should enjoy it."

"We need to take advantage of our youth and do something."

"Isn't that what we are doing?"

"Not fully."

A noise behind us startled us, but it was only Dylan returning from the woods.

He laughed, "'cuse me, I was draining the main vein." His smile was on sideways. "You look serious. Are you not having fun, Nick? Alice?"

"No, I am." I said, and Alice added, "we are."

"So why the face of a mathematician?"

"We are trying to figure out the answer to the question, why are we all here?"

His smile widened, but still remained slightly off, "I guess to have a good time, right? Life is short and fleeting."

The answer bothered Alice, and the more I thought about it, the more I was bothered by it.

"Did you see I brought a whole case of High Life? The champagne of beer. I stole 'em from my step-dad, and he was so drunk on Sunday, he thought they fell off his truck. You need one."

I nodded, but Alice was in another mood, "no, thanks."

"Um, okay, they are hot; Do you care if I get some ice out of the house?"

"You know the rules, Dylan, nobody goes inside. How do you think we've been able to keep this secret from Mom for this long?"

"It's only me, and not the whole gang."

Alice's silence was her response.

"Hot beer gets you drunk quicker anyway; I am going to bring one for you. "

Dylan left, and the pensive face returned to Alice.

"You know all of this is magic in a bottle. We captured it, and we cannot waste it," Alice said softly but in my ear.

"Magic in a bottle? We are high school kids. What can we throw away, Alice?"

"Drinking hot Miller's is a frat boy activity," she snapped.

"That's a little harsh coming from the person who started all this."

"It can be something bigger than chugging beers."

"Lighten up, Alice"

"The world is ending. Aren't you the one who kept telling me that?"

"I have told you that for years, and you didn't care, but now you do?"

"I always cared, but what could I alone do about the end of the world?"

"It isn't the end of the world; the earth will be here for another ten million years or so, but yes, life on the planet."

"You know what I meant." Her words were sharp with her agitation.

"Isn't that even more reason to not give a fuck and drink beerr like there is no tomorrow, because, uh, there might not be a tomorrow?"

"And why won't there be a tomorrow?"

"I hope there will be," I said as Dylan returned and handed me a can of hot beer with a bubble in the side.

"This isn't going to explode, is it?"

"Naw, you gotta open it like this."

Dylan popped the top, and beer shot out. He quickly put his mouth on it and began to inhale the exiting brew. The fountain of beer leaked down his chin as he desperately tried to secure a seal with his mouth.

"Shucks, man, let me go get you another one."

"It's okay, Alice and I were talking about the end of the world."

"Oh yeah? Well, the fact that it is imminent is both frightening and welcoming."

"Welcomed?" Alice questioned, but she knew.

"We are the first generation of humans to openly embrace the end. We don't run from it, and we all agree it is coming. It's

Chekhov's gun; if you show a gun in the first act, it has to fire before the end of the story, and the gun shown is multiple nuclear missiles. Those are coming, but the collapse doesn't even have to be nuclear. Think about the Boomers, raised by war vets with "Duck and Cover" videos every morning; they ran amuck because they thought the world was going to end. Why should they care about the future when it won't exist. Only the future came, and it was what they created: the world on fire. They justify it because in the back of their minds, the end is still incoming. Anyone with half a brain cell in our generation can see this. The collapse has to come now because nobody did anything about it. Since we were kids our lives have been filled up with plastic bullshit so we wouldn't notice. That's the new American dream; raise kids on so many Marvel SuperHero movies with the shitty collectables that won't biodegrade for six thousand years placed in the middle of the extra large burger and fries combo so the children don't pay attention to what is really happening. The dream is just that, so we all go to sleep thinking a two bedroom two bath with a picket fence coated in toxic paint is the answer. The water is toxic, the food is damn near nuclear, and the healthcare to fix it costs enough to wipe a person out. It's all deep fried smoke and plastic mirrors that won't last the car ride home after you bought it. We all notice this shit."

Dylan hit the hammer onto the nail. It was a mixture of our conversations over the years, but he was wording it perfectly.

"Our 401k's won't exist, and our retirement plan is to buuuurn," Rex sang, but it hit the mood perfectly. Exel and I chuckled.

"So we are just going to welcome the end?" Alice asked.

"Welcome it or not, it is coming. The world is going to end, or at the very least it is going to get a lot worse. The best of times for humans is behind us. The only thing in front is a slippery slope until our extinction."

"Why?" Alice pried. She knew the answers, but everyone was gathering around, and she knew Dylan would deliver.

"Why? Why? Well, because of a lot of different things. I like to blame the corporations, but it probably goes back to those in power who gave the corporations more power than a civilian. The boomers accepted their fate instead of trying to fix it, and since they accepted it, they also contributed to it. If you have a leak that you cannot fix, and the ship is going to sink no matter what, you might as well pop the rum and drink."

"Good for nothing, Boomers," Rex added to his freestyle on the guitar.

"So it's the boomers or the corporations?"

"It's both."

"So you blame corporations for the eventual collapse of society?"

"Among others, I guess."

Dylan poured the remains of the can into his mouth, swallowed, and then added, "it's the beginning of the end."

"And how is the end coming?"

"If not by an accidental nuclear war, I would say climate change, global warming, however you want to word it. The world is heating up, and nobody cares. "

"What if people did care?"

"I don't think it would matter; if I try to stop my carbon imprint on the planet, and let's say I succeeded, right? So I die, and I have zero imprint made as an effect on the planet; it makes no difference."

"So?"

"Seriously, think about it; if I do everything to not fuck the world up, it doesn't matter. Big oil is still pumping at a record pace so Americans can fill up their SUVs; the factories are still polluting the rivers; styrofoam and plastic are still getting absorbed into every-fucking-thing. What's the point of me doing something? The coal is getting burned no matter what, right?"

"Watch this." Dylan placed his now empty can onto the ground, and stepped onto the can with one foot, placing the other foot up in the air like a flamingo.

"The entire system of the civilized world is built on a capitalistic house of cards. Not only is it all make believe, but those controlling the strings won't admit how vulnerable everything is because it would shatter what they have. If we just look at America, the electric grid, the supply lines, your phone, everything, it is all created to keep capitalism running and those at the top at the top. It is all designed to sell more products so the bottom line of the corporations continues to be profitable."

Dylan, still standing like a flamingo with his foot on top of the empty can of beer, put one finger up to hold his points. Every single Moonlighter stood around him listening.

"Okay so?" Exel questioned.

"Okay, so?" Alice asked as Dylan balanced with one foot on top of the can.

"The smallest break here, or just a small touch, will cause everything to crumble."

He moved his flamingo leg down and lightly touched the side of the can his other foot was standing on, and the can collapsed under him. It was crushed by the weight of his foot.

"See, when it's all working and running, it's as smooth as I was standing on the can," He bent over to pick up the can.

I reminded him, "You were barely holding your balance."

"That's exactly right, Nick, but to Goomba way over there, or anyone not really looking, I was fine until -" Alice cut him off.

"Until you made the wrong move and collapsed society."

"It wasn't even the wrong move. I didn't use force. I lightly tapped the can, and everything collapsed. Once it starts to go, nothing can stop it. And I wasn't using the strength of a nuclear bomb. It was a small touch that did the can in."

"Huh?" I was lost.

"It won't take much to disrupt society back to the Stone Age, but the problem is, we have much more than a light touch coming."

"That's an excellent point, and demonstration, Dylan."

"Bravo," Rex clapped his hands. I didn't even know he was paying attention. Weed smoke poured from his body, and he patted Dylan on the shoulder.

"You do understand?"

"Sort of," I replied.

"We cannot do anything about the incoming crash of society, so why worry about it?"

"We can't?"

"No, the lone person cannot do a thing about it. Now, I am going to get you and me a beer."

"Yes, but what about a group of people?" Alice asked and stated.

"It depends," Dylan answered.

"Yes it does, Dylan. It depends on the people."

"Not just the people, Alice," Dylan answered.

"Right," Alice nodded.

"It depends on the people, and if they are willing to do whatever it takes to make changes."

"Yep, and doing whatever it takes means anything," Alice added, and a light bulb ignited over her head.

We were all in agreement standing around them, but we didn't think we could do anything to make a difference.

CHAPTER 11

The light bulb ignited over Alice's head turned into a fire, it ran rampant through her mind all weekend. It was Derby weekend so we watched the festivities on the local news with pure boredom. Mom was working OT, and the end of the school year was approaching, with finals that the teachers insisted we study for.

Watching the red carpet live as stars arrived was food for a nap, but as I snoozed, Alice watched as a protestor tossed red paint all over the dress of some famous reality star.

"Ha!" Alice cackled loud enough to wake me up.

"What?"

Opening my eyes to the ending of the ordeal, a news anchor, acting so important and righteous, informed me what I slept through.

"That young woman will spend the night in jail."

A female joined him, saying, "That was just uncalled for and mean! Her outfit has now been ruined."

"That's not a bad idea," Alice snickered.

"Didn't you hear him? She will spend the night in jail."

"Is going to jail not worth standing up for what you believe in?" Alice asked.

"It depends, I guess."

"Depends on what?"

"It depends on what I believe in, and how long I am going to jail for, I guess."

My answer didn't have a lot of thought behind it, but Alice nodded like it did. She was in a full brainstorm of ideas, and I didn't have a clue.

"Yeah, you're right," She added, but I knew something else was up.

"So you want the Moonlighters to attack the Kardashians with paint?"

"Of course not, and what would that accomplish?" Their clothing is sponsored; they're probably changing into the next designer outfit anyway. It is only a minor annoyance for them."

"Okay, so what, we take the paint cans to Wall Street? Or even better, we go to Washington and start puddling politicians with paint! I call dibs on the Turtle!"

I was awake now, a smirk on my face, but Alice wouldn't leave her mind.

I sat up, "No, I got it! We bring back tar and feathering people."

"Bigger."

"What's bigger than tar and feathering?"

Alice nodded, but I couldn't read her mind.

"The guillotine?"

"Hmm," I put a new idea into her head.

"Alice, we cannot bring back the guillotine," I reminded her.

"We can, but that's not exactly what I have in mind."

"Okay so?"

"You're not going to like this, but…"

She was wrong; I did like it, but I didn't know if the other Moonlighters would.

CHAPTER 12

"Banksy is a fraud; No, what's a better word?"

"Fugazi?"

"Fugazi? What's that mean?"

"It's like a fraud, I guess," Goomba answered Dylan.

The night started late because of a torrential downpour that flooded the area. Alice opened the garage, and we started inside. Dylan started harder than most, and Alice was questioning his future. His father's footsteps led to resentment and cirrhosis of the liver.

"Well, what is worse than a fraud?"

Goomba shrugged, "I don't know."

"What was I talking about?" Dylan questioned. He was eager to hear his own voice.

His beer wasn't empty, but he popped open another one before Goomba answered.

"Banksy."

"Yeah, right, Banksy is a fraud. He brands himself as this activist, right? He claims to be anti-capitalism, but at the same time he sells his semi-creative artwork to private millionaires for extortionate amounts, and nobody calls him out on it. It should devalue his whole message which is full of hypocrisy."

"So he's not a fugazi; he is a hypocrite?"

"Exactly!"

Exel smashed his cigarette into Dylan's empty beer can, "he does it for the money just like everyone else."

"Right, but none of us go around acting like we don't do shit for money; we work for money, but Banksy's whole message is this anti-capitalist, and then he -"

Goomba cut him off, "So he's a hypocrite, but who cares about Banksy besides wanna-be hipsters?"

"Wanna-be hipsters? You can't be a wannabe if you are a hipster," Dylan snapped.

And back and forth they went; it was another Thursday night. Alice welcomed us, we'd dare the newbies to drink a bottle of purple stuff, and we'd discuss similar issues. Discussing and debating on issues was how we could find things out. If we all just turned to our phones, we'd get trapped in echo chambers, and we might not ever come out.

The debating and informing each other was fun, but Alice was ready to take it to the next level. I agreed that her idea was interesting, but that was at the idea stage; it wasn't something that would become a tangible act.

Alice wasn't forceful, and she didn't demand anyone do what she said. That's why even I was surprised when it was unanimous to follow her.

"Nick and I have asked ourselves, why are we here?"

"It's all relative," Exel snarled.

"Yes, it is, but I have to ask you all, what is our purpose, and I do not mean in life, I mean here right now as the youth of this country, the Moonlighters who gather every Thursday night. Why do we gather?"

Jackson blurted, "I love coming here."

"Yes, we all do, but what happens next? Next year when we go off to college, or we take jobs to build a career. What happens?"

Dylan raised his hand but spoke before being called, "We will be even closer to the collapse if it hasn't already happened."

"Yes, Dylan, and what do you think will cause the collapse?" Alice asked.

"If I knew that I might be a rich man," Dylan laughed, and others joined him. "You know that's right!"

"We don't know, but if we had to guess what do most of you think it might be?"

"Nuclear war!"

"Climate change."

"A pandemic!"

"Famine likely from global warming."

Goomba raised his undersized arm before speaking; Alice pointed at him, "Yes, Goomba."

"By my calculations, climate change, or global warming, or as I like to call it, the climate crisis, is the only event guaranteed to end mankind, but other stuff like, you know, war or an asteroid, could end it. A famine would likely be caused by this global climate crisis, and that could very well spur another pandemic too, but the root or stem cause would be directly from the weather changing because the Earth is heating up from fossil fuels."

"How do we know the earth is heating up from fossil fuels?" Joey questioned.

Goomba turned to stare him in the face, "Because 99% of the

scientists say it is true."

"What about the other one percent?" Joey asked.

"They are likely taking a pay check from big oil," Goomba answered.

"Do we know the truth?" Joey questioned, but he wasn't asking Goomba now; he was asking all of us.

"Yes, I think we do."

"I've heard differently," Joey barked back.

And if it wasn't for Alice, we would have heard Joey's side, and perhaps some would have been moved over to it because that is exactly how the world worked. Alice was ready for it, and she wasn't going to let things go the usual route.

She began to hand out packets of papers. It contained proof that big oil lied, and reports from top scientists that the warming of the earth and the incoming climate crisis was in fact man made.

"Joey is the only one who seems to differ on our stances, but after reading this, if his mind isn't changed, then we can talk."

Only the flipping of pages was heard for a few moments before Dylan raised his hand and spoke, "First thing I want to say is I believe climate change is real, and I think it is because of fossil fuels, but this paper doesn't prove it. It doesn't have opposite sides, you know?"

"Opposite sides?" Goomba asked, but it was Alice who wanted to speak.

"Yeah, like we should hear from both sides and then decide."

"The opposite side of the truth is a lie," Alice cut through the other voices as they began to wonder too. "I am not here to argue what is fact or fiction. The top scientists in the world aren't conspiring!"

"The opposite side of the truth is a lie," Joey repeated.

Everyone shut up and pondered it.

"We can bicker here all summer if you want. Every Thursday night we can continue to this horseshit while stealing Robitussin and drinking hot beer until we are all thirty-five years old, or," Alice paused to let it sit in with us.

We were all eagerly awaiting her next words.

"Or," She paused again before breaking into her planned speech, "We can make a difference in the world. We either become the old generation that dies off from the climate crisis, or we become the young generation that saves the world. So, Moonlighters, tell me, what shall we be?"

"Let's save the world," Joey said, and we all howled at the moon in agreement.

CHAPTER 13

When Alice gave her speech and asked us to vote, the Moonlighters had 24 official members..

"Do something now as a young generation, inspire others, and make a difference, or grow old as the world burns and die a suffering death."

Joey's hand shot up first, and it wasn't because he liked Alice, he did, but this was because he was moved and ready to make a difference; his enthusiasm didn't sway when Alice broke down her plan.

Joey sat center stage, on his left was Cherry, her big, bulgy, beautiful blue eyes popping out; she was on the opposite side of Joey, but the spectrum wasn't vast. Cherry nodded with timidness, but Joey was ready to start the action because he was the one kid who really still thought he was the star of the movie. It was a gift and a curse. Joey grew up like that, and changing it would be hard. Alice didn't want him to change because she wanted to harness his energy.

Cherry was hip to everything, and that's how she entered our club. She became a Moonlighter because despite being beautiful, she didn't like people at her shitty high school in the southend. They were bigots, and she wasn't despite most of her family being red. Her mom raised her differently, and we'd all heard about the Jim Morrison tattoo across her mom's chest, but also how she made Cherry different from the rest of the family.

Cherry would bicker at us about her mom's tattoo, "the lizard god isn't even a good nickname for a rockstar!"

She was raised in the southend, but she wasn't a stuck up redneck who thought all folks had it equal. That's how most rednecks were; they assumed because they were poor that they poor black folk in the west end should shut up about it.

"My family thinks the poor white and the poor black folks are the same like we all got the same deal, but getting free ice doesn't mean the same thing when one side is getting frozen water in the winter, and the other is getting it in the summer."

Her voice was thick with a southern accent, but she was smart beyond her years; she was open minded, and beautiful to boot, and that's why we adopted her as much as she adopted us.

"Even my uncle with his college degree and all the property he owns is still a dumbass. He is living proof that you can go to college, even a big college on a big campus like he did in Lexington, and he can still be a bigot. He cheated his way through college, and didn't get his mind opened at all. That's why college is broken. You don't go to college to learn like you used to, but you go to learn how to get a career, or at least that's what my momma says."

Cherry's mom had raised her to know that going to college was a must, but it wasn't because she wanted her daughter to open her mind. She merely wanted her daughter to have a good paying job so she wouldn't have to live around the rednecks in Okolona.

Cherry was second to vote, and we all voted the same way. We were eager to follow Queen Alice on her mission.

After the voting, Alice gave another prepared speech, and she left us with words to think about, "We might become heroes, or we might end up in prison for the rest of our lives, and it might happen even if we are successful." She glanced around at all of us before she finished.

"So go home, and sleep on it. If you aren't down, then do not come back tomorrow night."

"Tomorrow? Do you mean tomorrow or next Thursday?" I questioned.

"Planning for something like this will take every night," Alice answered sharply.

"Mom will be home tomorrow night."

"No, Mom is camping this weekend."

"What about those that don't come back because they aren't down? I am down; I am down like a car with four flats, but I mean maybe others," Dylan asked.

"Those we do not wish to partake even though they voted, well, they can obviously come back on Thursday's because we welcome anyone here on Thursdays, but they might overhear something because we need all the time to plan."

"So they shouldn't come back?"

"They can, but they might be held liable because we will be discussing plans."

"So they shouldn't?"

"Dylan, are you coming back tomorrow or not?"

"I am, but I am asking for everyone else."

Alice turned to the rest of us, "Moonlighters, we are going to change the world!"

We howled, and I screamed, "change the fucking world!"

We danced under the moonlight and around the fire, beating our chests like small King Kongs.

CHAPTER 14

I know Alice gave us a day to think about it, and I did. I'm sure the others did as well.

When I woke up, Mom was awake, sitting on the couch with her camping gear ready to go by the door.

"How did you sleep?"

"We don't have school today," I replied.

"I know that, silly goose; come here and give me a hug."

The dim stench of Marlboro's thickened the air around her.

"You stink, Mom!"

"Oh, come here and give me a hug; are you going to be okay without me?"

My head was still asleep, "What do you mean without you? Because you smoke?"

"I don't smoke that much, boy, I mean this weekend when I am camping with Earl."

She tried to tickle me, but I yanked her arm away. I was too big for her now.

"You are getting so tall, but I swear, you will always be my little tickle monster!"

"Mom, stop it!"

"Oh, you stop it!'

I smiled and sat down next to her on the couch; even as an 18-year-old, I loved Mom's attention. I shrunk on the couch next to her, sliding my legs out to slouch. Not uttering a word, my mind was filled with Alice's words from the night before. It was a lot to take in, and I was barely awake, but Mom knew something was up.

She tried to tickle my ribs as she asked, "what's wrong, Tickle-Bug?"

I moved her arms away, "nothing, Mom."

"Oh, it is something; you don't think I know my own son?"

"It's just something Alice said, but nothing major."

"Oh, Alice, huh? What did Alice say?"

"It doesn't matter, but Mom, is Alice older or am I older?"

"What do you mean older?"

"With twins, like, one has to come out first, right?"

"Oh, so you and Alice are twins, huh?"

"Mom, stop being funny!"

"I believe you were here first, and then Alice came, right?"

"How would I know?"

"I'm sorry, Tickle-Bug!"

She went back in for the ribs and stomach, and she got me. I didn't laugh, but I arched my back and pulled away.

"Mom!"

"Sorry, Tickle-Bug!"

"You do know that tickling is a sign of abuse, right? Do you tickle Alice like this?"

"If Alice was here, I would."

"Whatever, Mom."

"What did Alice say that put you in such a bad mood?"

"It's nothing."

"It's not nothing."

I shrugged.

"Tell me, Nickalous."

"Nothing. She just said that sometimes people have to do things they don't like in order to get things accomplished, and that even great people like Martin Luther King and Gandhi had to do stuff they didn't like in order to get goals accomplished."

"Well, I don't know a lot about Gandhi, but MLK did, and he was murdered for it."

"A lot of great people have been murdered, and Alice mentioned that too. Sometimes bad people are evil, and they just do bad things because they want to, but everyone usually justifies what they did; one way or another."

"Alice told you all this?"

"Some of it, and some of it I came up with because of what she said."

"And what did she say?"

"No, nothing, really, you know?"

"No, Nick, I don't know. What did she say? She's talking about MLK and Gandhi; what exactly did she say?"

"I told you; it was about doing things you do not want to do in order to get things accomplished."

"And what are you trying to accomplish?"

A horn went off coming from outside.

"Earl is here."

"Earl can wait."

"Does he not come in and get you anymore? Some date, Mom!"

"Oh, hush it, you know he has a bad knee."

"A bad knee? It seems he is just an asshole."

"Oh, whatever Nick, you won't tell me what Alice said, and I have to run."

"If Alice was here she would probably tell you; that is how she's been lately."

"Well, is she here now?"

"No."

"When will she be here?"

"I don't know, Mom, geez!"

"Okay, Nick, I love you, but I have to run."

Earl knocked on the door, but opened it before he was invited inside.

"Pam, hey, hello, are you in here; Are you ready?"

"Yes, I am, sorry."

"Hey, Nick, how is everything? Your mom and I are going up to Nolin Lake; you wanna join us?"

"No, but I will help Mom carry her stuff out because I know you got that bad knee."

"Bad knee? Shit, boy, I don't got no bad knee, but if you wanna carry it, shit, less for me, kno'what I'm saying?"

"Yep, I sure do, Earl; you are saying you're an asshole, and you honked because you didn't even want to help Mom with her stuff."

"Nick," Mom smacked my arm.

Earl was dumbfounded, but he often is.

"What in the hell is that supposed to mean?"

"Nothing, Earl. I am just joshing with you."

"Yeah, Nick is in a bad mood because Alice put some words in his head," Mom made a wheeling motion around her head with her hand to let Earl know I was crazy.

"Shit, Alice was here? Maybe she shouldn't come 'round here if she gonna make you mean, Nick."

"Earl! We need to go! Nick, I will grab that!"

Mom grabbed her bag, and rushed Earl out the door before one of us said something out of pocket..

Earl was an asshole, but Mom was fine with it. He treated her okay for the most part. He didn't beat her, and he brought her flowers on her birthday and Valentine's Day which is what women want.

On the counter Mom left me a note, and in the fridge she left food. I devoured it all for breakfast, and I went looking for Alice.

CHAPTER 15

"X will be here shortly, and he can get us what we need."

Alice was jotting in a notebook.

"Do you remember who is older?"

"We are twins."

"Yeah, but like who came out first?"

"You did."

"How do you know?"

"Because I remember."

She didn't take her eyes off her notebook.

"Sure, Alice thing; why is X coming?"

X or Xavier joined our ranks through the nineteen year old hippie named Rex. Rex played guitar, wrote folk songs, and smoked weed. He graduated from Atherton at seventeen, and he'd been roaming Bardstown Road for two years until he found us. X also went to Atherton, but he lived down in the west end; somehow his grandmother's property in Portland curved into Atherton's district which meant he and Rex rode the bus together.

X was as sharp as a tack, but he detested going to school.

"I never fit in because I didn't play sports. If you're black and don't hoop, you're an outcast. I didn't see what the big deal was, a second grade game of throwing a ball through a hoop. There wasn't much to it, but I wasn't interested in it."

X's sister, Bella, appeared a few times, and while they were both fantastic dancers, they also wanted to blow up the entire system. "Shit, I was born with that desire!"

The chiming of our doorbell startled me, but Alice kept her nose buried in her notebook.

"I guess I will get that."

X and Rex entered our house for the first time with a foul aroma of overstuffed ashtray.

"So the guy is going to meet us, and everything is set up," X informed me.

"Okay, so should I get Alice?"

X and Rex crossed their eyes, "uh, no, it's probably better that it is just us three."

"I don't really feel like going, though."

X questioned my response without saying a word. His face said it all.

I shrugged, "fine, but let me tell Alice I am leaving."

Rex reached out, "dude, it is okay; we are all nervous, but let's just go and get this over with, okay?"

X whispered, "You got the dough?"

Reaching into my pocket, I felt the money, "yeah."

"Okay, let me do the talking, this guy is a friend of my cousins, and he ain't always on the up and up."

X drove his mother's car, and the nerves between Rex and X were palpable. It was making me nervous so I asked them, "why y'all so nervous?"

"Shit, you know why, man, come on," X replied. X dressed like a prep; he wore bright polos and khakis that set off his dark black skin. His connection was a cousin, but his nerves informed me he wasn't close to this family member.

The shotgun house in the older part of Portland should have been demolished, and we pulled up right in front; X parked on the street, and told Rex to wait in the car.

"I'mma leave the keys in here so once we go inside the house, you need to move the car to that alley over there."

"Why?" Rex wondered aloud.

"Because it's hot out here."

Nerves crept into my belly as we approached the house, and my palms began to sweat. We boycotted the front door on the porch, and instead ventured into a side door.

X knocked, and a tall skinny black man wearing a wife beater opened the door; before he acknowledged us, he turned and yelled, "Tell J his cuz is here."

"Tell that faggot to come inside," a voice yelled, and it was more than a cause for concern.

Stepping through the side door, the house was dark and quiet; another black man wearing a Spongebob t-shirt entered from a room in the front of the house.

"What's up X-Xavier," he said with extra annunciation on the X.

"Oh, hey man, this is the guy I was telling you about Nick."

Reaching my hand out to shake his as X continued, "Nick this is my cousin," but his cousin cut him off as he shook my hand. "J, J-Will; that is all you gotta call me; everyone calls me J-Will."

X shook his head, and then he nodded his head.

"Very nice to meet you."

"Yeah, so X-Xavier tells me you are looking to buy a llama."

"A llama?"

"A biscuit? A piece, right?"

"A biscuit?"

The tall man wearing the wife beater shook his head, "A gun, nigga, Jesus!"

"Oh, yeah, right."

X lowered his head, "Two of them."

"Yeah, and you know the ticket right?"

"Ticket?" I asked.

X turned to me, "the price."

"The price tag, damn this dude isn't a cop is he?"

"No, I ain't a cop!" I shot back sharply.

"What in the fuck you need a gun for?"

"Huh?"

J-Will shook his head, "You ain't gonna shoot up a school is you?"

"No," X answered.

"Hell no, man, hell no," I responded.

"It's you weird ass white dudes that shoot up the schools; you know even the hardest motherfuckers in the hood, the killers of all killers don't even shoot up the schools."

"Shit, if anything, we tell the kids to go home before it gets to popping!" the other brother added.

Vigorously I shook my head no, "I'm not shooting up a school. I am not shooting up anything."

"Yeah, well the numbers been ripped off, and these ain't loaded."

J-Will tossed back a cover from the coffee table, under it were two handguns.

"This is the beretta nine and this is a four-five. No numbers and no bullets."

"Okay," I reached to grab the nine.

J-Will smacked my hand, "need the paper before you touch it, blood."

"Oh, right," I pulled out the wads of hundreds in my pocket, and handed it over.

"Five hundred; okay, you can touch them, but let me tell you this, white boy, if you do shoot up a school, you better off yourself, or I will find you in prison and have you raped with a razorblade dildo, and Smurf here will kill your family and your dog."

X chimed in, "dang, even his dog?"

"I don't have a dog," I responded, but it wasn't the right response. "But I am also not shooting up a school, I promise you that. This is just for protection and hunting."

Smurf in the corner with one leg on his jogging pants pulled up laughed, "Hunting! This white boy is dumb."

X moved towards the door, "We gotta be heading out."

I moved towards the door too, but I was carrying both the guns like I was leaving the house with flowers.

"Nigga, you gotta put those guns away!" J-Will snapped at me.

"Oh, right," I responded as I stuffed one down my pants, and then tucked the other under my shirt, holding it in place with my armpit.

"Thanks again, guys!"

We stepped outside, and the door slammed shut the instant we did.

"Where is the car?" X asked.

"You told him to move it; look, there it is."

As we scurried to the car, X looked at me, "I guess you got my answer."

"Answer about what?"

"Whether I was down for the cause or not."

CHAPTER 16

Alice wasn't around when I got home so I hid the guns in the garage.

Clark showed up first; his BMW had the drop down, and I raced through my mind to remember how Clark became a Moonlighter. He was friends or cousins with Aurora, and she brought him into the group, but I didn't know much about him. He was flamboyant as all get out, dressed like a prep with a sweater over his shoulders. His attire was always the same yet the clothes were always different which meant he wasn't flipping the same shirts with new sweaters; Clark was exiting a beamer. He was a loaded, country club kid, who bought new white shoes when his old ones got scuffed.

He walked quickly into the backyard, and approached me as soon as I stepped outside.

"Alice, I have to say, I do not know if I can partake in any violence or illegal activities; it is bad enough that I have acted improperly here, and with X and Exel, and well, whoever, but if my daddy found out I was partaking in anything even remotely close to the Thursday night trips, I would lose everything."

"Uh-huh," I nodded.

"So Alice, listen,"

"Nick, I am Nick."

"Oh, right, so is Alice not here yet?"

The backyard was dark without the fire, but I was clearly Nick.

"Have you been drinking or smoking?" I questioned.

"No, not yet, I just wanted to inform you."

"I can let Alice know, but we will miss you, Clark."

"Oh, I do plan on coming, on Thursday nights, you know like you, Alice said, right?"

"Sure, I guess, but why are you so scared of your old man?"

"I am not scared, but my parents provide for me. I am going to UK in the fall, and they are providing money for my living situation, and I do not want to jeopardize that. I will have my own house in Lexington."

"Oh, but what would jeopardize that?"

"My parents are Republicans and Catholics; they don't condone any of this!"

He was frantic like his parents might be watching from across the street through binoculars.

"I will let Alice know."

He didn't answer me; he looked at me with a confused look on his face, and then he came in and gave me a hug.

"Sorry, I am sorry. I don't know what I am doing, but I know I cannot get in trouble. I love you, Alice, Nick. I love you for doing this, and I love you for having me over, and I will never forget, but right now, I need to to just go to Starbucks and get a -" Tears streamed down his cheeks as he backed away.
"Goodbye!"

Rushing to his car, he didn't even look back until he was driving away.

Alice opened the backdoor, "Who was that?"

"Clark."

"What was that all about?"

"He's not joining us so our number is 23 if everyone else comes."

"That's a big if," Alice responded; she closed the door and walked back into the kitchen.

Opening the door I asked her, "Where have you been? I put the guns in the garage."

She was gone when I entered the kitchen so I went into the living room, but she wasn't there either.

"Alice?"

The light was on in the attic so I walked upstairs; Alice was sitting at the desk copying notes into a notebook from something on the laptop screen that we shared.

"Did you hear me? What are you doing?"

She didn't respond.

"Alice, did you fucking hear me?"

"Huh? No, what?"

"I hid the guns in the -"

"In the garage, I heard you!"

"Why did you say you didn't hear me then?"

She didn't answer.

"What are you doing?"

She didn't look up, "planning."

"Planning? So the guns are in the garage, but I really didn't like going over there."

"You didn't have to go; X would have gone by himself. He got the other guns without a problem."

"What other guns?"

"The ones under your bed."

Alice still wasn't looking at me, I dropped into the pushup position to look under my bed, and there was a stockpile.

"Holy smokes, Alice, what is all this?"

"Some of that was already there, remember? You were stockpiling for the end of the world."

"I had canned goods and water filters, not rifles and handguns; what in the hell, Alice?"

"We aren't stockpiling for the end of the world anymore, Nick."

"No, it looks like we are stockpiling for World War Three!"

"We are stockpiling to save the world."

"How are we going to save the world?"

She didn't answer, and my eyes jumped out of my head.

"Is this a hand grenade?"

"Jesus, Alice, what in the actual fuck?!"

She still didn't look up.

"That could detonate and blow me up while I am sleeping; is that active? Tell me that isn't active, and it is some sort of prop you bought at the Army Surplus store."

"It better be active for the price we paid for it."

"Holy mother of - you know what, Alice, I am on Clark's side here. We cannot have a grenade and guns. Is it active or live or whatever or just an old one that won't blow up?"

"If you wanna make an omelet you gotta break some eggs."

"Jesus," I backed slowly away from it. "Are we making an omelet?"

She was still marking in her notebook, and mostly ignoring me. I rolled towards her side of the room, and glanced under her bed.

"I don't see anything under your bed; I am actually surprised I'm not seeing stuff to make a bomb."

Pulling myself up using her bed, I asked her, "Can we keep the grenade under your bed?"

"It won't go off unless you pull the pin."

"How did you get the grenade?"

"Cash knew a guy, or maybe it was Jackson," She finally removed her head from her notebook, and she pondered where the deadly hand grenade came from with a pen in her mouth.

"Oh, so now you don't remember who provided the grenade, huh?"

Her head went back to her work. "Can we talk about it later? I am busy right now."

"You are busy planning, but can I ask what part the grenade plays in the plans?"

Finally, she glanced up at me, "Didn't we talk about it?"

"No, Alice, I'm sorry we didn't freaking talk about the grenade part of the plan!"

"Operation FDIC."

"F, D, I, C? What the heck does that spell, FDIC? F-dick?"

"Yeah, I don't like the name either; we can still change it. Do you like Operation Roosevelt better?"

"Honestly, I don't like any operation that involves a freaking grenade!"

"We almost went with Operation Glass-Steagall, but that was a stretch."

"I don't know what that is, and I am afraid to ask."

"Yeah, FDIC is gonna stick. It's part of the endgame, but we are calling it phase two right now."

"What are you looking at?"

As I tried to glance at the screen she shut it.

"People are starting to show up; we need to go outside."

She stood up, and pointed outside; a few people were starting a fire, but I couldn't tell who it was through the window.

"Can we remove the hand grenade and keep it in the garage?" I asked, but Alice was gone.

CHAPTER 17

"That's inhumane!"

Rex was correct, but it was a cart before the horse issue. I was worried about everything that would happen before it became inhumane to the folks in the hospital.

"Hospitals have generators; my mom is a nurse; they have power outages all the time," Richard chimed.

Richard was a Hoosier from Floyd Knobs; the first sticky part of Indiana after New Albany. "We escaped from the inner workings of Indiana; the real bad parts where you cannot stop if you are a minority," Richard joked to us when he first admitted where he was from.

"He ain't joking. They used to have signs, but now we all know not to stop in any farm looking spot in Indiana," X added.

Every joke has a little bit of truth to it.

Richard didn't fit in from first grade on when his classmates played smeer the queer with him every day at reccess. We were all happy to welcome him and his sister into the Moon Gang.

The topic of discussion this evening was the hospitals. Rex wondered if it was inhumane to deny power to folks inside the hospital.

"Yeah, but those are power outages for hours; they cannot sustain for a long time without power. People will die," Rex stated.

"How many will die if we don't?' Alice snapped back.

Rex shook his head, "we don't even know if your plan will work so you are talking about killing people for sure versus maybe saving the lives of, well, of a lot, I guess."

"This plan would save humanity and life on Earth," I reminded Rex.

"Could," Rex wisely reminded me.

"What if we provided them a way to keep the electricity on, but only them?" Dylan asked.

Joey nodded, "I don't think it works like that, but if they use generators we could provide them with gasoline."

"How much gasoline would we need to provide them with? And how would we even provide it to them?"

"Somebody would come along and steal the gas," Xavier added.

Alice's brow furrowed, but she didn't take long to respond, "we will provide them with a way to get electricity."

"How?" I asked.

"We will set out solar panels and batteries. We can provide it, and we can place it on the roof of these hospitals, and they can have an electrician come and set it up."

"How in the hell are we going to get solar panels?" Rex questioned.

"Solar panels are expensive; we don't have the budget for it," I reminded Alice.

"Budget?" Dylan laughed.

"We can steal them," Joey responded.

"How?" I asked.

"Steal them, duh," Exel's sister Brandy informed me.

"Right, but from who?"

"Solar panels are guarded pretty heavily because they contain a lot of silver," Jackson informed us.

"Well, it is only day one of planning; we can figure it out," Alice stated.

Alice wrote in her notebook, and then turned to the white board hanging on the panels of the garage as if the problem would work itself out down the line.

"That does move a few things around as far as importance," Alice said, but she was speaking to herself.

I wasn't going to let it slide, "we cannot just steal solar panels, and provide them to hospitals, and tell them, if you want to keep people alive, here you go!"

"Why not?" Alice asked me.

"Why not? Because!"

"Because, why not?"

"Alice, are you insane or crazy? We cannot throw solar panels on top of the roofs, for one, we don't even know how many solar panels we need to provide, or how many batteries, we don't know any of that shit!"

Joey answered me, "It won't be that hard; my uncle installs solar panels for a living up in Indy; I will get a hold of him, and I will ask him. It's not that big of a deal."

"It is a minor speed bump, but it will be handled," Alice informed me very calmly.

"Minor?"

I questioned everything, but only said the minor part out loud.

"We have already decided to move. It's a can of worms now."

Turning to look at the 23 Moonlighters in front of me, it was hard to not compare them to kool-aid drinkers. They all hung on everything Alice said, and they were ready to attack the devil if needed. Yet, here I was drinking it too.

"So is everyone down?" I yelled.

Collectively, they all glanced around, and nodded that they were.

"I mean, are we freaking sure? This is some heavy metal shit; spend time in prison, right?"

"We are all here, and we had a day to think about it," Dylan snapped.

"Yeah, but why?"

Rex spoke, "Why what?"

"So everyone here is down to become anarchists, but why?"

"It's not anarchism; sure, the chaos theory applies later, but this isn't anarchy," Rex barked.

"You are the one who convinced us," Joey responded. He was staring at me.

"Yeah, you did!" Brandy added.

"I convinced you? And how in the hell did I convince you?"

The group all glanced around, and now it wasn't just Joey wondering why; it was all of them.

Goomba was the first one to say, "You showed us everything. Before I started coming here, I didn't know about the climate crisis, or what a BOE was, or how much plastic was spreading. There isn't rain water anywhere in the world that isn't contaminated."

"You made me hip too," Rex added, but Goomba wasn't finished.

"I think what got me was when you told me that microplastics were everywhere and they were even being found in placenta and in baby poop. That is unreal, and you were the one who told us about the mass extinction. You explained it all to us, and now you are questioning us?"

Goomba was right. I did tell them everything I knew about the incoming collapse, but I didn't think anyone would do anything about it, and I definitely didn't think it would be us.

"That's what this is all about; we are the Moonlighters, and we are going to save the day!" Joey added in typical Joey fashion.

I nodded, but quickly shook my head, "one person, or one group of people cannot save the planet."

"We aren't one person; It is 23," Brandy confirmed.

"23 people cannot stop it either!"

"That is why what we are doing is about inspiration," Goomba reminded me.

"Inspiration?"

Joey stood up, his blood was flowing now, "Yes! We are going to inspire thousands and perhaps millions!"

"We might, but what if we don't? This isn't a movie, Joey. We will spend the rest of our lives in prison."

Joey was amped, and the rest of the group began to show emotion too. Alice's head was inside her notebook; she was ignoring it all.

"This is all insane," I muttered.

Alice turned to me and spoke, "The gesture of the solar panels can really set up the next part of my plan. Can we get another hand grenade?"

"I think so," Jackson answered.

"Even if we don't; I know how to use that one for max value," Alice was excited. She turned and walked to Cherry to speak with her.

"You brought us in, Alice, and we believe in you," Joey rubbed my back while he said. Cherry was next to me, and she nodded yes. The fire was still bright, and the reflecting eyes staring back at me was cult-like. It was a cult willing to do whatever Alice said.

CHAPTER 18

According to Alice, we were ready two weeks later.

"Fourteen days isn't enough time; we aren't ready," I informed her, but she didn't care.

"This was your idea in the first place!" She finally answered.

"My idea? Are you freaking nuts?"

Not only did she not care, she wasn't listening either.

"How in the hell was it my idea?!" She was on the laptop, so I slammed it shut.

"You better hope the screen didn't break." She opened it to check, and it wasn't.

I made my way downstairs while exhaling heavily. She was aware of my annoyance and the fact that this was not my idea. I began descending the stairs but stopped halfway down, turning around and returning up.

"No, it was not my idea; this was clearly your idea!"

The room was empty, the window was open, and the curtain was flapping in the breeze. She'd somehow exited the window onto the roof. I shouldn't say, somehow, I knew how; I used to smoke out there; I just never knew she went out that way. I stuck my head out, but the top of the garage was empty. She'd managed to jump down, and I wasn't that crazy.

Slamming the window shut, I turned to read through her notes. The laptop was open to a page about Mill Creek, and she'd written the notes in my handwriting.

"What in hell…"

I couldn't understand why she used my handwriting; she had her own. It was for plausible deniability or some other reason I didn't know.

She was ascending the steps as I was making my way back to the window.

"Thanks for locking me out," she said with a half finished smoke in her hand.

"First, I didn't know you smoked on any day but Thursdays."

"We don't hang out any day but Thursday."

She sat down but quickly noticed her notebook was turned towards me.

"Yeah, I read through your notes. Why are you using my handwriting?"

She turned the notebook back towards her without even looking up at me, flipped to a page in the back with a drawing, and began comparing it to the laptop screen.

I was tempted to slam it down again, but instead I grabbed the tippy top, and moved it slowly down until it was closed.

"We aren't ready; fourteen days isn't enough. Not even SEAL Team Six could get ready to do this in two weeks. I will not let you go forward with this. "

"With what, Nick?"

"With this fucking insane mission you conjured up out of your, well, out of your I don't know what!"

"This was your plan, remember?"

"How was it my plan?"

"You were the one who put the Moon Gang together. Every single Moonlighter came here because of you, and they all come every Thursday to hear you preach about how the end of the world is coming unless we do something. That is you, Nick!"

"The end of the world *is* coming, but we can't stop it!"

"If we cannot stop it, you shouldn't have preached it every Thursday!"

"I don't preach it every Thursday!" I snapped back.

"Oh, okay, Nick, so after I welcome everyone to your Gay Fight Club, what do you do?"

I shook my head.

"You bring up a new end of the world scenario, and tell us that we are the only people that can do anything about it."

Her voice was rising, but I didn't respond with anything but a "uh-huh, sure thing."

"Oh, don't give me that Nick! How do you say it? People need to act now, or else, blah blah blah," she made air quotes with her hands and deepened her voice to sound like me,"it's like when you are in traffic, you don't realize you *are* the traffic! Or whatever in the hell you say!"

She was testing me, but I didn't know what her point was.

"I don't know."

"What do you mean you do not know? You say the same shit every week with a new example, and then you say that there isn't an army of aliens coming over the hill to save us from ourselves. How do you say it? Only life on earth can save life, and we are the life!"

It was the first time I'd seen her mad in years.

"So now you are suddenly scared? We are ready to fight your war!"

"My war?! This isn't my war!"

"You're the one who brought all the facts to the table every week, and kept pushing for us to do something. What did you think would happen?"

"I don't know, I guess apathy like every other human-being on the planet!"

"Oh, that is rich, Nick! Apathy! You've been pushing us to the ledge, and now that we want to jump, you want to put on a parachute?"

"I didn't push anyone to the edge!"

"Bullshit!"

Her phone vibrated on the desk between us; it was Goomba calling.

"Why don't you pick it up and ask him!"

"Ask him what?"

"Ask him why he is doing this. No, ask him why he keeps coming back. "

"Okay," I said, and I snatched her phone.

"Hello?"

"Hey, Alice, Nick," Goomba questioned.

"It's Nick," I informed him.

"Okay, Nick, so I have done everything I can, and put all of it onto the USB, but the," his voice was whiny, and full of eagerness, but I cut him off.

"Tell me why you come over on Thursdays."

"What do you mean?"

"Why did you come over every Thursday?"

"Uh, because it was fun."

"It was fun? Is it not fun anymore?"

"No, it is, but what do you mean?"

"Who pushed you to do this?"

"Pushed me to do what? Come over on Thursdays?"

"No, Goomba, answer me, was it me or Alice that made you do whatever it is you are doing."

"What? When?"

"You know what I am talking about? This plan! Alice's plan, why are you doing it?"

"Because nobody is going to do anything. The corporations control the narrative, and the -"

"Okay, yeah, I know the shtick, but tell me, why are you doing it? Did Alice convince you or did I?"

The silence on the phone said everything as he thought and slowly stuttered out the words to answer me.

"Uh, I don't know. Is that a trick question?"

"No, answer it. Did Alice convince you like she did everybody else, or did I convince you to carry out this plan?"

"Which plan?"

"Which plan? Which plan are we working on?"

I glanced at Alice for something, but she rolled her eyes, took her half-smoked cigarette, and opened the window. Looking down at the notebook, I saw Alice's handwriting as she'd scribbled in bubble letters, "Operation Midnight."

"Operation Midnight."

"Operation Midnight?" Goomba repeated.

"Midnight is a vital plan that needs to happen, and to quote you, midnight is the first step to save life on the planet. Humans need to do something or else, and we aren't the or else."

"Midnight will save life on the planet; did I say that?"

"Yes."

"So answer my question, Goomba, did Alice convince you like she did everybody else, or did I convince you to carry out this plan?"

"Is that a trick question?"

"Is it a trick question!"

"Okay, I am sorry, Nick. No, Nick, I am talking to Nick, right?"

He was confused because he called Alice's phone, but I answered, and we do sound similar on the phone; multiple people have said it.

"This is Nick! So answer the freaking question. "

"I came into the Moon Gang when you asked me, Nick. I believe in everything we are doing, and I know that even my life can help save the future of life on the planet. "

"So I asked you, and not Alice?"

"Yes."

"Okay, but it was Alice who made you want to carry out this stupid Project Midnight thingy, right?"

"Operation Midnight?"

"Yeah, whatever," I answered, but glancing around, Alice was gone. The window was closed so she must have bounced downstairs with her head between her legs because she knew what Goomba was telling me.

"It was you that I believed in; Alice or Nick or whatever, I am a Moonlighter, and I am here to light the fire with my presence."

He was speaking nonsense.

"Did you already take Tussin?"

"No, I haven't touched it since you told me not to touch it."

"You are speaking in tongues; when was the last time you tripped on Tussin?"

"Not since you made us all stop so we could work."

"Work? Stop? How long?"

"Since March."

"March?" I questioned.

"Yeah, I guess."

"So nobody is using it every Thursday?"

"No."

"And you are ready to carry out Midnight because of me?"

"Yes, humans created this mess, and humans must fix it. "

"Because of me and not Alice?"

"Uh, yes, because of you."

Now I needed to think, so I paused.

"Why did you call me?"

"I completed it. The USBs can interact with any computer they are plugged into, and it wasn't that hard. We send them out as winners, people love to be winners; and if one person enters it into a work computer, boom, we got 'em! "

"And what if I told you to stop?"

"Are you telling me to stop?"

"Yes, fuck yes, I am, Goomba! You are talking about hacking someone with a USB! That is illegal, and not just illegal but highly illegal. We will all go to prison!"

He didn't answer me.

"Hello?" I asked.

Goomba's voice was full of confusion, "yes, so you are asking me to stop?"

"YES!"

"Okay," he responded, and I heard the nerves in his throat.

"Okay, what? Are you going to stop?"

"No."

"What? And why not?"

"Moonlighters are unstoppable. We know forces will try to prevent us from carrying out our mission, but we must do it regardless. It might be our own families, and it might be other Moonlighters, but we must continue moving forward because life on the planet depends on us. We are brave scientists who understand the data and realize we need to act; we are the modern day monks, but instead of lighting ourselves on fire to burn in protest, we will create a massive protest as we light a fire with our presence until we die. The Moonlighters are fighters, and so we fight! Many will try to stop us, but nothing can. Moonlighters are unstoppable."

It was a speech that Alice had written and handed out. I knew exactly what it was, but still I replied, "what are you talking about Goomba?"

He didn't respond, and he hung up the phone.

"What in the hell is going on, Alice!"

I announced her name again as I ran downstairs, "Alice!"

CHAPTER 19

"Alice? Hey Nickie," Mom said as I reached the bottom of the stairs.

"Mom, where is Alice?"

"I don't know, Sugar Bear, why don't you tell me?"

"Mom, I really need to talk to Alice!" I insisted.

"Okay, Sugar Bear."

As I glanced around, looking for Alice, she wasn't downstairs so I headed back up to the attic.

"Is everything all right?" Mom inquired. "Is there anything you'd like to discuss with me?"

"Yeah, I am fine; I need to talk to Alice."

"Do you want to tell me what this is all about?"

"No," I yelled as I rushed up the stairs.

Alice was back at the desk, staring into the laptop.

"What are you doing now?"

She asked me, "What did Goomba say?"

"You know damn well what Goomba said!"

Mom was still on my case; she'd followed me upstairs, "Nick, is everything okay?"

"Mom, I told you, everything is fine."

Mom began to glance around the attic, "Who are you talking to?"

"Alice," I responded.

"Oh, is she up here?"

"Yeah, right there," I said, pointing to the desk, but Alice was nowhere to be found; she was a damn magician, and I appeared to be a moron.

"Okay -" Mom said with as much astonishment as I had since Alice was gone.

The window was open again, but I couldn't let Mom know that we snuck out the window to smoke on top of the garage so I walked towards the window and shut it.

"Are you sure everything is okay?"

Turning to look at Mom, I noticed Alice had taken out a pack of smokes that I used back when I did smoke. She musta found mine, and been tempted to burn one. It wasn't the only reason I didn't want Mom in my room either; if she happened to look under the bed, it was crawling with guns and ammo and who knows what else.

"I need to get something to drink; Let's go downstairs."

"Okay, Sugar Bear," Mom responded, but she stopped, as she noticed dust near the floor by my bed.

"You need to vacuum up here, Nick; look at that muck," she said, but she was halfway down the stairs and had a clear view under the bed.

"I know, Mom, let's go downstairs; my throat is parched, and I need some water. I will sweep and vacuum later."

"Okay, but look under your bed; is that dirt?"

"No, I will get it later."

I was attempting to stand in her vision, but decided instead to rush her downstairs.

She was clueless, heading right down.

"I gotta leave for work in a minute, okay, Sugar Bear?"

"Yes, fine," I replied.

Alice's phone vibrated in my hand. It was Dylan calling.

"Dylan is calling; I gotta take this, Mom."

"Okay, Sugar Bear, do you want me to bring you some water?"

"NO!" I snapped, but added, "I actually have a bottle up here."

"Okay, I am heading to work."

"Hello?" I answered the phone while backpedaling up the stairs.

"Hey Nick? Alice?"

"Yeah, it is Nick, I have her phone."

Alice was climbing back into the window.

"I got cars, and the new tags. It should be just enough of a -"

I cut Dylan off, "Hey, Dill, let me call you back or have Alice call you back in five minutes."

"You need to stop closing that window," Alice yelled.

I fell to the ground, and looked under the bed but it was empty. All the guns were gone. I ran to look behind the Christmas decorations, and all the stuff was gone too.

"What did you do with all the shit?"

"What shit?" Alice questioned before repeating, "did you hear me? Stop closing the window."

"Where are all the guns?"

"The guns are in position. Was that Dylan on the phone? Does he have the vehicles? If he does, well, the guns are being loaded into the cars."

"Alice, what are you talking about? It doesn't matter what Goomba said, we aren't going through with this!"

"You're right; it doesn't matter what Goomba said."

"Jesus, Alice, are you insane?"

Alice turned to shut the window, and Mom yelled up the stairs, "I am leaving for work, Sugar Bear; Try to get some sleep; Goodnight!"

"Okay, bye Mom!"

"I love you, Nickie," She said, and I could sense her eyes staring up the stairs at me waiting for an answer.

"Alice is here now, Mom; she was sleeping or hiding behind the Christmas decorations."

"Okay, I love you, goodnight."

"Have a good night at work; I love you too Mom."

"I was sleeping behind the Christmas decorations?" Alice asked with an attitude.

"I couldn't tell her that you snuck out the window to smoke; could I?"

Alice sat back down at the computer, and I ran to the window to watch Mom back her car up.

"You look like Malcom X," Alice informed me as I pulled the blinds down.

"Yeah, well, I am not Malcom X, and you aren't either, so whatever we have to do to call this off, we have to do it."

"You're right because Malcom X is dead; he was killed by the government just like Martin Luther King was."

"What?"

"The same government leading us into fascism and the end of the world."

"Oh, great so we are fighting fascism now?"

"You bet we are!"

"No, no the fuck we are not!"

"The Moonlighters are ready, Nick."

"The Moonlighters? The Queer Moon Gang is ready, huh?" I barked at her.

"Yes, but remember, Nick, we can call ourselves, Moonlighters, the Queers Under the Moon, the Gay Fight Club, it doesn't matter, but the mission is moving forward. You cannot stop it. Everyone is prepared to move forward even if you try to stop it."

"Oh, so now we have a few rifles and no training, but you think we are ready for your dumbass Operation Midnight?"

"Everyone has training," Alice added, "and everyone knows their role."

"Training with guns?"

"Nick, we are kids from Kentucky, 80% of us grew up shooting guns."

"Not us, Alice! Mom got rid of Dad's guns a long freaking time ago!"

"Yeah, well Dylan knows how to shoot, Joey does, even Goomba has shot a gun before," Alice snapped back, but she wasn't looking at me now.

"Shooting a .22 in the woods doesn't equal being ready for this," I pointed at the words on her notebook that read, Operation Midnight.

"All operations are moving forward as planned."

"No, no they fucking are not!"

"You cannot stop it, Nick, but you can try. Here, why don't you try. Call Dylan and tell him to stop it."

She handed me her phone.

"Sure thing!"

I dialed his number, it rang twice, and Dylan answered, "Hello."

"Dylan, it is Nick. I am calling it all off. All of it."

"What?"

"You heard me, okay?"

Dylan didn't respond, and Alice stared at me with her green eyes and her arms folded in front of her.

"Dylan, listen, I am calling it the fuck off! It is over! Do you understand?"

My blood was boiling.

"This is a test, right? Dylan asked.

"No, fuck no! This isn't a test; I am canceling it all. All of it, Operation Midnight, and everything else," I tried to read through the notebook, but it slipped and fell to the ground. "All of them are canceled!"

Dylan didn't respond.

"Did you hear me? Call everyone, okay? Call all the Moonlighters and tell them it is over, okay?"

"Do I need to remind you that Operation Midnight is vital?"

"Vital? Vital to what?" I asked.

"Vital to saving life on the planet," Dylan said, but Alice mouthed the words as if she knew exactly what he was going to say.

She did know.

I shook my head at Alice while responding to him, "No, dude, just no."

"I am a Moonlighter, and here to light a fire with my presence."

It was the same exact words Goomba had used.

"Nope! Not even a little bit, Dylan. It is over. O-V-E-R! Did you hear me?"

Dylan was quiet, and Alice was gone.

"Dylan?"

He replied with the exact oath like words that Goomba had.

"Moonlighters are unstoppable. We know forces will try to prevent us from carrying out our mission, but we must do it regardless. It might be our own families, and it might be other Moonlighters, but we must continue moving forward because life on the planet depends on us. We are brave scientists who understand the data and realize we need to act; we are the modern day monks, but instead of lighting ourselves on fire to burn in protest, we will create a massive protest as we light a fire with our presence until we die. The Moonlighters are fighters, and so we fight! Many will try to stop us, but nothing can. Moonlighters are unstoppable."

And then he hung up.

CHAPTER 20

The headlights were dim, but that was the least of my concerns. I drove it into my side yard, and the lights illuminated the presence of a bunch of Moonlighters. I was driving one of four cars Dylan was able to obtain for Operation Midnight, a white 2004 Lexus.

Dylan shrugged when I asked about the driver's seat being ripped down the middle.

"It looks like someone hid drugs in the seat, drove the drugs back from Mexico, and then instead of getting the stuff out like they put it in, they just took a knife and cut it open," I said after he shrugged.

"Yeah, it does, doesn't it?"

It wasn't the response I wanted.

"Where'd you get these?"

He was holding license plates and a screwdriver, and about to change all the plates. He'd waited until I returned so the gas station camera would pick up the old tags.

"I don't remember which one is for the Lexus!" Dylan's anger returned.

Goomba heard him, and yelled out, "L! The one with the L on the back is for the Lexus!"

"L, thanks," Dylan replied. "So each car will have a stolen tag that matches the car. The fuzz can run tags without even moving; the cars have that equipment in them so we will look like cars that aren't stolen, but just because of the tags."

"The fuzz? Nobody says, Fuzz anymore. Did you just read The Outsiders?" Devon joked.

"I read it in middle school," Dylan answered.

"Yeah, so did everyone else, but that book was written 70 years ago."

"So what's the new term for the fuzz or the police?"

"Them boys, or boys in blue.."

"Five-0."

"Twelve."

"Fuck Twelve was one of my first bands," Rex responded.

"I always liked squalie," Devon said.

"Po-po," Cash suggested.

"The po-po? No, never say that, Cash. How about One Time?" Devon asked.

"One time? What is that from?" Cash questioned.

"I don't know. I think it's from old heads talking like, 'man, this one time -"

Devon, Cash, and Dylan all cut up to that one.

Dylan used the screwdriver to remove the original plate from the Lexus.

The other three vehicles weren't nearly as bad. There was an ugly Camry that used to be tan but was now turning brown, and a Ford Focus with a crack in the windshield and a stench so bad that Exel got into it and immediately jumped out.

"Rex is gonna have to drive that one," Exel barked.

Rex gave a nod. He was strumming his six-string guitar and singing a song he wrote about what was about to happen, or perhaps it was about what had already happened. It was similar to the song made famous by Israel "IZ" Kamakawiwo'ole, but instead of singing "Over the Rainbow," Rex sang "Somewhere Over the Haywire."

It was fitting; we were definitely well over it.

The final vehicle was a black pickup truck, but the black appeared to be spray painted on it. It had black rims that appeared to be spray painted too, as well as a dark tint. Exel didn't want to drive that either.

"It's too small, I want to drive the Lexus," Exel remarked.

"The headlights suck on it," I responded.

"Yeah, I don't care; there is nowhere to put my shotgun in this truck," Exel snapped back.

"I can hang my old man's gun rack up in the back; he don't need that shit, and even if he does, fuck him!" Joey cackled after he said it.

Joey was checking the tires; his sister wasn't around. She was smarter than he was.

Rex continued to sing and strum.

"Oh, somewhere over the haywire
Blue birds die
And the dream that you dare to
Oh, why, oh, why can't I?"

I was still vehemently opposed to the whole thing; Operation Midnight was a bad idea, but that wasn't why I was still here or what irritated me. I was irritated because no one was nervous, and the atmosphere was so relaxed that it was difficult to digest, but I figured everyone thought it was a joke, and the mission would be called off at any moment.

Everyone was nonchalant; Rex singing, Exel upset because he couldn't hang his shotgun, Goomba telling us to not put the stolen license plates on yet, Joey was checking the tires, Devon and Richard's sister Tiffani were loading backpacks into the back of the truck, and Alice was still upstairs combing hair or something.

Xavier showed up with Steven's sister, Jane, and they rushed over to me.

"We couldn't get it," Xavier whispered, but everyone heard him.

"Couldn't get what?" I asked.

I'd been staring up at the window above the garage for an hour waiting for Alice to come down, but she was still up there trying to get herself pretty.

"We couldn't get it," Xavier repeated.

"Okay, well, I guess we will have to do without it; fucking-A Xavier, I don't know what else to tell you," I snapped, but I didn't know what he couldn't get.

"What about that part of the mission?" Xavier asked.

Jane was close to him, and I knew they were dating, or messing around, but she was oddly close to him.

"Jane, where is Steven?" I asked.

She gave me a confused look before making eye contact with X.

Xavier answered me, "What are you talking about? Are you okay?"

Rex sang new verses, and I turned to bark at him, "Rex, can you not play that song over and over?"

Cash yelled at me, "Hey, I like the song. It's relaxing."

Jackson chimed in before I could say anything, "Yeah, it was relaxing; why you being a dick to everyone, Alice?"

"I'm just nervous, look, I think maybe we shouldn't go through with it tonight," I said it with half meaning it, and halfway not meaning it all.

"It's a test; remember, other Moonlighters might try to stop us, but the mission must go on!" Dylan screamed.

"Yeah, a test," Exel said, and then Jane repeated it.

Xavier came in close to my ear, "Cherry is ready, and she understands her assignment."

"Where is she?" I asked.

"I cannot disclose that information."

My voice rose, "What do you mean? Tell me!"

Rex halted his strumming.

"I know this is a test too. I will get my team ready for phase one. Cherry is ready for phase two," Xavier said, and then he headed towards Exel to see what car he was driving.

Goomba pulled out two golf bags full of golf clubs, and brought them over. They had a zip cover, and he undid the zipper. Inside three rifles were poking out.

"The handgun is down here in this compartment," Goomba said as he opened it. Inside was a pistol.

"Jesus, holy Mary," I said.

"Yeah, we are armed up, but I wish we had more. Should I give them out?"

"Not yet; we should do another vote. Who wants to do another vote?”

I wasn’t just stalling, I was also trying to figure out how to make it clear to everyone that this was an insanely bad idea.

X approached me, leaving Jane with Devon.

“It’s hard to tell if you are testing us, or if it might be something else, but we are commit at this point so stop fucking playing.”

His voice was the deepest I’d ever heard him use. He was ready, and so was everyone else.

Exel yelled, “It’s time! Either you come with us, or you know what we have to do.”

I didn’t know, but Alice would.

I backed away from everyone as they stared at me, and I opened the screen door to the house.

“I’ll be right back,” I jumped into the house.

“I gotta tell Alice something. Two minutes, tops, be right back!”

CHAPTER 21

"You need to leave," Alice said as soon as I arrived upstairs.

She was facing away from me, looking at me through the mirror she sat in front of with a brush in her hand.

"I need to leave? We need to vote."

"We aren't doing a vote. I hope you didn't announce that there should be a vote. The Moonlighters are ready to go, and if you try to stop them, well, you know what happens."

Her eyes were large, drawn up by her raised brows.

"No, Alice, I'm not sure what happens," I replied, walking over to the window to look out.

Alice didn't answer me.

As I gazed down into the backyard, I began to count everyone.

Dylan was talking to Joey, but Wanda and Chloe weren't around; Jackson was smoking, but Amber wasn't around. Exel was counting shotgun shells on top of the truck, but Brandy wasn't around. She'd been gone for weeks. Jane was still standing by X, but Steven wasn't around, and Bella was missing too. Devon finished loading the car, but Danny wasn't around. Tiffani, who had helped Devon, was on her phone, but her brother, Richard wasn't around. Rex, Cash, and Goomba were bullshitting about the guitar. Cash's sister Auroria wasn't around.

Cherry wasn't in the backyard either. Our numbers had deflated

"Cherry is in position, or at least X said she was," I informed

Alice.

She didn't respond, and I noticed the notebook on the desk.

"Our numbers have decreased," I explained.

"No, our numbers are fine besides Clark, everyone is accounted for and ready to move," Alice finally said.

I left the window, and flipped through the notebook before responding.

"That's a lie, and you would know the truth if you went down to see everyone. Richard isn't here, Auroria isn't here, Steven isn't, Bella isn't; You don't have a clue, Alice!"

A stopped flipping the notebook at a page with groups written at the top. It was my handwriting, but I didn't write it.

"This says Richard, Brandy, Jane, and X are in Group A. That will be difficult because two of them are not present. That is why we must hold a vote! We need to reach a consensus."

Alice stood up, "The blue dress is a symbol as much as anything to the Moonlighters."

"Are you fucking listening?" I snapped.

"Everyone here has felt safe since we started our Thursday nights, and every Thursday I wore the blue dress."

"Alice, who cares about a dress; we need to schedule a vote right now, and cancel your stupid, Operation Midnight, or else someone is going to get hurt, or locked up for the rest of their life, or worse, okay?"

"You wouldn't think a blue dress would symbolize anything."

"There was that movie, The Devil in the Blue Dress; Maybe it symbolizes that?"

"Yet every week, I wore the blue dress, and everyone came back.

I wore it because it was easy on the eyes, and because I was Alice, leading them to their Wonderland. We create a safe place here in our backyard, but we cannot keep them safe forever."

"You're being a little crazy right now, Alice."

"This dress is from a Halloween store; it is an Alice in Wonderland costume actually."

"Okay, look, can you go down and lead a vote, or should I call the police? This has to end before something terrible happens."

"I bought two of the Alice dresses, and tried to stitch them together. I didn't want to wear an Alice costume."

"Alice, it doesn't matter. Only half of the folks are here, and I do believe that is grounds for a vote."

"I wasn't very good at sewing. It's hard, and I didn't want to mess up the dress. It was the only dress I owned."

"Alice!"

"As I learned to sew, and I still suck, but I wanted to put something very figurative on the dress. I would have to stitch it, and I am still new to stitching as well as sewing."

"This isn't the time, listen Alice, half of the folks did *not* show up; that is grounds for a vote or something!"

"The anchor symbolizes hope and security; which is what I wanted to bring to all of the Moonlighters, but it wasn't the right fit for us."

"Did you take a dose of Tussin?"

I walked to the window and looked out, but to my amazement, everyone who wasn't there a moment before, was now there. Chloe and Wanda were talking. Amber tossed a cigarette into the fire pit; Brandy was loading shotgun shells into the truck. Steven was flirting with Bella. Danny and Richard were talking in the far corner, and Auroria had joined them. Rex and Goomba were still bullshitting.

"Fuck me, I guess everyone is here, but that is even better," I hung the last part out in the air so Alice wouldn't focus on the first part.

I turned to her, "Everyone is here, so we should really do a recount, okay?"

"You said our numbers have decreased," she sang out in an exaggerated version of my voice.

"No. Yes. What I meant was we need to do a vote, and everyone is here now."

"So at the bottom of the dress, here," she was in front of me, pointing down to the large white part on her dress, but she was holding up a pillow to hide what was underneath it.

"I don't see how this is important right now. Wear the dress, or don't wear the dress, but we aren't doing Operation Midnight."

"I was going to put deer antlers on it, deer are a sign of hope, and that would be perfect, and it would look better than the anchor. People might not know what an anchor represents, but again, I didn't think it fit us.

"Alice, what in the fuck?"

"So what are we?"

"What are we? We aren't about to go carry out this mission, that is what!"

"No, seriously, tell me."

The pillow was still in front of her, and she was swaying her left leg with a child like glee.

"I don't know, Alice, we are the gay fight club or something else? What? Can you tell me?"

"Yes, I thought about that, and the rainbow, but the rainbow is happy. We aren't happy, are you happy, Nick?"

"I was until you started taking everything and making it so serious, and you started plotting out insane plans that cannot work!"

"Yes, I didn't think so, and the rainbow is played out, but what are we?"

"I don't know, Alice; we are the Moon Gang, right? We are the Moonlighters so you drew a moon?"

"I didn't draw anything," She responded.

"I didn't mean draw, look, it doesn't matter, but what?"

"I stitched it," she said somberly.

"Okay, you stitched a moon."

"A moon isn't the sign of a rebellion."

"Well, what is the sign of a rebellion?"

She dropped the pillow, "an owl!"

"Wait? A sign of a rebellion, so now we are a rebellion?"

"Look at it!"

Stitched into her skirt, was a black owl; its claw with three points in a rage was poking out. It was detailed, and impressive. The owl was vicious.

"It looks ready for a fight."

"Not a fight, a rebellion."

"Right, but -"

"Nick, no but, this was all your idea. All of it. One person cannot do anything, we have people, and our actions will inspire more people."

"I get the idea; I truly do. I understand the sentiment, but even if we succeed, then what?"

"You understand that it's not about our lone success here, right?"

I was quiet and staring into the eyes of the owl on her dress.

"It's time for a rebellion, and a rebellion will lead to a revolution, and that means change. Change doesn't happen at the voting box, and it doesn't happen unless action is taken. We are taking action, and you, you are the night owl who will lead them."

"I can't," I replied. My eyes fixated on the owl; it looked alive.

"You are the only one who can."

"How can I lead them? Who am I?"

"Why don't you tell me who you are."

She was slowly moving her dress, which caused the owl to move; I took my gaze away from it and looked at her in the mirror.

"Who are you?"

"I don't know," I responded because I didn't know.

"Yes you do, and before you go downstairs and tell everyone, I want you to tell me."

"I am the night owl."

"Yes and?"

My gaze returned to her dress and the owl on it. It felt like a dream, but it was a dream I'd had before.

"I am the vicious night owl, ready to attack!"

My blood was picking up with adrenaline.

"And!"

"I am the vicious night owl, ready to attack with the Moon Gang by my side!"

Alice was behind me, her hand on my shoulder, and her face on my other shoulder as she looked at me in the mirror.

"And?"

"I am the vicious night owl, my claws are ready to attack, as I am ready to attack with my gang, the Moon Gang by my side, and I am ready."

I pounded my hand into my other palm.

"Ready for what?" Alice asked, she was giddy.

"I am ready to lead a rebellion that will inspire a revolution. A rebellion that will inspire millions."

"So who are you?"

"I am Alice."

PART TWO

"Over the Haywire"

CHAPTER 22

There was blood from the bottom of my dress to my forehead. I tried to wipe it off, but it smeared onto my hand and across my face. It wasn't supposed to happen like this.

As we approached the plant, it was illuminated and gave off an ominous vibe. The visual of the smoking towers with the dead of the night sky was apocalyptic. I was driving the Lexus and leading the X group. Joey, Jackson, and Goomba were with me.

We pulled into the plant, and a moving bar blocked our way. A fat guard stuck his out of the booth and informed us we couldn't go any farther.

"I need to turn around; I don't know how to back up."

"Well, I am sorry ma'am; I cannot open the gate unless you have an access code."

Joey leaned over me, and began exchanging "fuck yous" with the guard. It escalated from there until Joey jumped out brandishing a handgun. The guard tried to run, and Joey chased him.

I chased Joey.

The guard was fat and old enough that there was no way he was going to outrun Joey. But as Joey closed in on him, he turned and fired his weapon. I didn't even know he was carrying a gun; the bullet whizzed by my head like a lightening fast wasp, and I ducked way too late.

The shot was awkward, clumsy, and not as loud as it should have been. It happened fast, and then things slowed down as I fell to the ground.

Joey began wrestling with the guard, and got the piece away from him almost instantly. I was on the ground, but when I turned back, I saw Jackson was on the ground by car. Jackson and Goomba were out of the car following us. Goomba stood shell-shocked by the hood of the car, and Jackson fell back into the front bumper and slid down.

The bullet entered his chest area and didn't exit. They fell down immediately, and I went into shock with them. I fell down onto the ground, turned back, and saw Jackson laying on their back.

"Oh shit," Goomba whispered as he ducked behind the car. "Pressure on the wound," Goomba muttered, but I understood him.

The procession of time slowed back down as I put pressure on Jackson's chest.

A punching sound repeated over and over as Joey bashed in the guard's face filled the dead air since I couldn't speak. Jackson's eyes were looking at me but staring beyond.

"It will be okay," I said as I put both hands over his wound.

It wouldn't be okay; Jackson was dead.

"Holy, holy, fuck, fuck, fuck," Goomba belted out as Joey approached. He was dragging the guard, and had a gun pointed at his head.

"Get up, Jackson," Joey said. Then he ordered it, "Get the fuck up, Jackson!"

Joey took the gun off the guard, who was crying, and he poked his head close to Jackson's face.

"Jackson is gone," I said as I stood up; my hands were soaked in blood.

"Gone? No, what the fuck!" Joey smacked the guard across the back of his head with his pistol.

"Stop, please, I have a family," the guard fell to his knees.

"Oh no," Goomba stuttered and walked away from us.

Joey kicked the guard in the back. "Jackson right there is our family, asshole!"

"Calm it!" I snapped. Someone needed a calm head, and I knew it wouldn't be Joey but I was in charge.

"Put him in the trunk."

"What no?" The guard said.

"No," Joey said, and Goomba repeated it.

"It's either shoot him or put him into the trunk."

"Let's shoot him," Joey said through their clenched teeth. He placed the gun close to his head.

"Shit's real now," I said to myself as I clenched my fists. We had fucked up.

"No!" The guard yelled a few different times as he fell to his knees.

"Trunk him, now!"

Joey grabbed the man by the back of his collar, and yanked him up.

"What about Jackson?" Goomba asked.

"Uh, I don't know, I guess put them into the back of the trunk too."

"He is dead," I reminded Goomba, but the words hurt after I said them.

"Maybe he's not," Goomba said.

Joey snapped at the guard, "Get in!"

"No, wait, have him carry Jackson," I ordered. "Shit just got real," I muttered under my breath.

Goomba removed the contents from our trunk, placing them into the backseat.

The guard struggled with Jackson, but eventually got them into the trunk with Joey's help.

"Get in too," Joey pointed with the pistol.

"No, he is bleeding," the guard answered with his hands up halfway.

"I don't give a flying fuck, buddy, get in the fucking trunk or I will shoot your kneecaps with your gun!"

Joey had the guard's gun in his waist, he removed it, and pointed it at him.

"Okay, okay, okay," the guard jumped into the trunk of the Lexus, and Joey slammed it shut on top of his head.

Joey repeated different renditions of, "Fucking, motherfucker, fuck!"

"Shit just got real!"

The car fishtailed on the gravel as I put the pedal through the floorboard driving towards the front of the building.

There wasn't a soul in sight, and we were supremely lucky no one was watching the cameras. The sun was close to rising, we were behind schedule, and Goomba reminded us of another problem.

"The two shotguns are in the trunk."

"Fuck!"

"Why didn't you take them out with the other shit?"

"I wasn't thinking!"

Joey leapt from the shotgun seat, dashed to the back, and took a position over the trunk.

Joey returned to the front, saying, "Pull it open, I'll stand by the side, and if he has it, I'll shoot him. If he doesn't, I'll aim it at him, and you, Goomba, come around and grab them."

As I gripped the steering wheel, wet blood dripped across it.

"What's the deal?" A voice pierced the darkness.

"Shit!" I exclaimed.

"Oh, hey, there, you know that fat guard that was up front?" Joey asked.

"Yeah, Tommy Boy?"

"Yeah, well, it appears there was an accident," Joey tucked his gun into their waist in the back, while approaching this person.

"Oh, shit, that's wild because I thought I heard a gunshot. Did he faint? He mighta had another heart attack; Gosh dang it," He shook his head hard, and turned to grab a phone on the wall behind him.

"I will call an ambulance; Y'all ain't supposed to be even in here though. How'd y'all see him from the street?"

"We had a flat tire, and came in because -" Joey cut me off.

"Get your hands up!" Joey removed the gun swiftly and without warning.

"Oh, shit, okay!" He shot both hands up like it was noon on a clock, and dropped the receiver. It dangled and crashed into the wall.

He was a tall man, at least 6'5 so we couldn't put him in the trunk even if we had room.

"Tie him up," Joey barked at us.

"The zip ties are in the trunk."

"Tie me? Why?" The man asked. His hands were still up, but he didn't want to be tied up.

"The zip ties are in the trunk with the shotguns and the fat guard," Goomba reminded us.

"Fuck!"

"Y'all got Tommy in the trunk? That cannot be good. Whatcha want, huh?" His arms were lowering as he asked.

"Get Tommy out, get the zip ties, get the shotguns, and let's tie Tommy up with this man. What's your name?"

"Ted."

"We aren't asking names, remember!" Goomba reminded me. It had been my idea, I didn't want people we might have to kill to be real to us.

Jackson, on the other hand, was very real. It didn't register that they were dead.

I wasn't thinking, popped the trunk, and Joey screamed, "No!"

The guard in the trunk popped up like an obese Jack in the box; his face covered in Jackson's blood, and he was gripping one of the shotguns. He was struggling to get out of the trunk, and Joey rushed back to him and slammed the trunk back down on his head.

"Damn, Tommy Boy!" Ted said, but then he turned to either grab the phone or run. He did a stutter-step like he was trying to figure out which one to do, and then he just stopped.

"Freeze!" I yelled at him, but I wasn't holding a weapon. It didn't matter he froze.

Joey slammed the trunk down on the guard again, but it wouldn't close because the shotgun was poking out.

The guard clicked the trigger, but it wasn't loaded.

"It isn't loaded," Goomba informed me as he stepped out of the car.

The guard kept pulling the trigger, and Joey continued to slam the trunk on his head.

"It ain't even loaded," Goomba yanked the shotgun out of the trunk as Joey slammed it one last time and it shut.

The guard yelled, "I got another one in here!"

"Shit is real!" I said. "Joey, the other guy," I pointed at Ted.

"I ain't going nowhere. Whatcha want anyway? Money?"

"No, we don't want money. Money! Money is what got us here!"

"Money is what got y'all here?" Ted asked. His accent was thick as his glasses, and his glasses looked like the bottom of a vase.

"I'm going to open the trunk, do not point the shotgun at us. We know it isn't loaded," Goomba was speaking through the trunk.

"The bullets are in here, somewhere, I know they are."

"The bullets are in the backseat," Goomba said.

"I found one," The guard said.

"No, he didn't," Goomba said. "Pop it."

I popped it, and the Jack in the box shot out with the sawed off shotgun in his hands. This time, he wasn't trying to fire it;

he tried to use the butt of the gun as a weapon. He aimed it at Goomba and swung, but Joey slammed the trunk down, and the guard's fingers were caught in it. He screamed, and Goomba yanked the gun out.

Goomba slowly reached into the backseat, pulled out a box of shotgun shells, and loaded the gun as if he had done it every day since Kindergarten. He walked slowly back to the trunk, pointed it at the guard who was clenching his broken fingers, and he shot him point blank.

"Jesus!" I snapped.

The blast was deafening; Ted dropped to the ground.

"Why'd you do that?" Joey questioned.

"He killed my friend," Goomba responded. "Come here, you aren't getting the bullets; we are tying you up."

"What in the hell did you shoot Tommy for? Y'all related to the dude messing with his wife that he called the law on for -"

Joey cut him off, "Get over here!"

Goomba dropped the gun.

Ted tucked his head low, and walked towards us, "Okay."

Goomba sat back down in the backseat, reached over for one of Jackson's smokes, and lit it up.

The sawed off shotgun was hot and laying in the gravel, but I ran to pick it up.

Goomba sat in the backseat of the car smoking and crying, and repeated my words, "Shit's real now."

Joey tied up Ted, but he was too big to put into the trunk. I grabbed the golf bag out of the trunk, and put the handgun into my pocket.

All three of us were covered in Jackson's blood. Joey forced Ted to walk in front of us into the building; his hands were tied behind his back with zip ties

Shit was real now.

CHAPTER 23

"Now what?"

The building was very loud, with various humming noises all over it. Hard helmets were required by law, and another notice warned us that we were in a restricted area. We didn't know how lucky we were that the cameras weren't being watched.

Ted led us into the main area of the building. We were carrying backpacks full of canned goods, and each of us was armed. Goomba, was done crying, and pointing a sawed off shotgun at the ground in front of him; Joey's weapon was a black double pump.

A skinny older man with glasses on was asleep in the main room of the building.

"Damn it, Curtis, I was hoping you called the law," Ted said; his voice woke the man.

"Huh? Why?"

Ted shook his head, "You in here sleeping Curtis!"

"Naw, I wasn't," Curtis replied. "What's going on?"

"Get your hands up!"

"Get the zip ties," I told Goomba.

Goomba pulled zip ties out of his backpack.

"What in the hell is going on?"

"They shot Tommy," Ted informed him quickly and matter of

factly as if he was saying "Tommy fell asleep on the job," and not discussing a murder.

Blood was still visible on all of us.

"What? Why?"

"He shot our friend first," I said because if we were going to state facts, I wanted that known. Jackson never hurt a fly.

"Wha -?" He couldn't finish the word.

Joey approached him quickly, "Now stand up, and shut it off."

Curtis stood up slowly with his hands up in the air, "Don't shoot me! Shut what off?"

"Shut off the power."

"What?"

"Shut it all off."

"What?"

Joey leaned into the man with his gauge pointed right at the man's nuts, "did you not hear her? She said to shut everything off or your nuts will get bucked."

His legs shrunk inward to guard his junk, "I can't just shut it off."

"Why not?" I questioned.

"Why not? This is a coal power plant! If I shut it off, power will go out across, well, across half the state!"

"Not half the state! It's not even a quarter of the state," Goomba said sharply.

Joey cocked his weapon, and drove it into Curtis' pants

"Shut it down!"

Ted shook his head, tears rolled down his face, "You better do it,

Curt. Tommy is dead; they ain't messing around."

Behind the man were four TVs with live camera feeds from around the plant. We were lucky Curtis was asleep, or the police would arrive.

"Alright, alright, I will shut it off," Curtis belted out in a high pitched tone.

I sat down at his chair as Joey followed Curtis into another room.

"Shut that shit down," Goomba yelled at Joey as they left.

"Where is the backup generator for the plant power?" Goomba asked Ted.

"It's outside. It's already hooked up, gassed, and all that. I am the one who checks it weekly to make sure."

"So how long will it last?" I asked without looking back at him.

"The generator? It's gonna last about eight hours on four or five gallons of gas."

"How much gas do you have?'

"There's a bunch out."

"How much is a bunch?"

"A few gallons poured into a barrel.."

"And these cameras here will stay on?"

"Yes."

Goomba pointed at the screen, "Who is that?"

"That's Walt; he always shows up to read the paper in the morning. He's the last of a dying breed."

"What?" I inquired.

"Walt, there, he is the last of a dying breed; I tell you. He shows up two hours early just to sit in the breakroom and read the newspaper. Old Walt should be retired, but he hates his wife, and would rather work than put up with her."

"How many people are working right now?"

"Walt ain't working. He shows up to read the paper."

I turned around to face Ted, "No, how many people are on the clock for the graveyard shift?"

"It's just us three," Ted answered. "We been understaffed since before the Covid thing happened, but since then we been real low on manpower. I was off nights for 17 years, and now they got me back working 'em." He shook his head hard back and forth.

"Yeah, all our data said three men," Goomba answered me.

"Goomba, go tell him to go home, and then it's your job to secure the front gate."

"No, Jackson was supposed to chain the gate up."

"Walt ain't gonna like being sent home," Ted cut in to add.

"I don't care about Walt!"

"Goomba go send him home, and then you will have to lock the fences so nobody else can get inside!"

"The chains are in Jackson's bag, I think."

"Well, where is that?"

"I could only carry my backpack," Goomba answered me. "His bag is still in the backseat."

"Fuck."

"You want me to tell Walt to go home?" Ted shrugged at our predicament.

"Yes, I do," I answered.

Ted's face shot back and a look of puzzlement grew over it, "Really?"

"Yeah. We aren't here to take hostages or kill anybody."

"Besides Tommy," Ted reminded me.

"He shot our friend first," I reminded Ted.

"Okay."

"It doesn't matter. Yes, go tell that man to leave, and you gotta leave too. If you want to live, you will go down to your car, and get out of the gate before Goomba locks it."

"Okay."

"If you are still here, I don't know what might happen."

"Shit, I won't be here! Can you get these off of me?"

"Don't try anything funny or you and Curtis and Walt won't be going home."

"Shit, I bet Walt would like that."

I stopped short of Ted with my knife out.

"I mean we won't!" He added.

I cut him free.

"Can I get my stuff out of my locker?"

"You need to be gone before the gate is locked."

Ted took off out the door, and headed towards Walt.

Goomba and I watched on the camera as he ran down a hallway, approached Walt, and then kept running. Walt turned around to watch him, and then followed him. It was obvious Ted was shouting at him.

"Go lock it up after they leave."

"I am on it."

"What about the other guy?"

"He is here in case we need him. That's what he gets for sleeping on the job, right?"

"Turn your walkie on."

Ted ran into the parking lot, jumped into his truck, and peeled off; Walt wasn't far behind him.

As the electricity briefly went out, I waited in the pitch black. Power was reestablished when the backup generator finally started. The cameras weren't back online, so the screens were black.

Part one of our mission was complete. The death of Jackson still hadn't hit me, though. I pulled my burner phone out of my pocket, and looked at the messages.

X texted me, *group A, mission one accomplished.*

Devon's message was similar informing me that Y group accomplished phase one too.

Dylan's message read, "Steven and I are in position. Let us know what you need."

I wrote in a group message, *Jackson didn't make it.* But I deleted it. They didn't need to know this yet, so instead I wrote, "We need more manpower here."

Dylan wrote back instantly, "On our way."

The black TV screen's reflection allowed me to see that my face was still covered in blood. I looked around for a rag to wipe it down.

The coal power plant wasn't producing power which meant thousands were waking up to find their electricity out. Goomba was locking the gate, and Joey was placing zip ties on Curtis' hands. Phase one was complete. I sat down, and began to question everything.

CHAPTER 24

Joey returned with Curtis, zip tied him, and stuck him into a hallway closet on the second floor. He unloaded the backpacks which were full of tasty MRIs and canned goods, and then he ran to open the gate when Dylan arrived.

Watching on the camera, Joey and Goomba stopped to talk, Goomba handed him a key, and they both went separate ways.

Goomba returned with Jackson's bag, and the small camera and tripod. I was going to send our message out, but my nerves were a wreck. I told Goomba to set it all up.

Goomba was breathing hard, and sweat fell from his forehead; he was holding his composure, though. At least better than I was, so I ducked into a side office, and closed the door before yelling back at Goomba, "Keep watching the cameras."

Closing the office door, I sat down behind a desk. There was a window facing west, and a picture below the window of a Karen-looking white lady holding a basset hound. Staring out the window, I could see the entire west end of the plant. Coal black smoke filtered out of the towers in front of me even though the plant was off, and gray clouds were approaching on the near horizon.

I sat down in the office chair, trying to find my courage, but when I swung it around, Alice was standing on the other side of the desk.

Remember as a kid when we'd drive by a big factory like this, and you'd tell Mom it was a cloud maker? Her voice was soothing, and her words took me back.

"Perhaps we've actually gone too far -" she cut me off.

What are you doing in here?

"Jackson is dead."

I know. That's why you shouldn't be here. You need to continue the mission so Jackson's death isn't in vain.

"All of our lives are going to end in vain! Goomba, Joey, Dylan, mine, all of us! I yelled as I slammed my hand on the desk.

You were always going to die; now your life will mean something.

"Yeah, well, I didn't -"

She cut me off again, your death might mean something too, but it doesn't matter. Rebellions need moments like this!

Her words cut through my thoughts. She was right; I was right. Jackson was dead, but it was an accident; the guard was dead too, but he wasn't supposed to be armed. None of that would matter to the jury and judge, and that is if we even got that far.

Dylan and Steven will be here soon, she said.

"Yes. That's good right?"

What do you think?

"What do you mean, Alice? Just say it because obviously, I don't know."

She lowered her chin like an adult talking to an infant that was acting up. What?

"You wanted Joey; he is here, but now they are both here."

They are both here?

"Yeah, did you think Dylan wasn't going to do everything he could to get back here with you?"

They all were.

"No, none of them were supposed to make it back. Did you think Dylan's feelings for you just disappeared? He is here because he thinks he loves you."

She answered no, but I knew she meant yes.

"You know it is true; how come you never told him about Joey?"

She exited now as only a reflection in the bottom of the window. Her response was harsh and to the point, I didn't need a reason to tell him.

"You didn't need a reason, but you also didn't tell him. And you didn't tell him for a reason."

She was behind me now, shaking her head.

"Nothing will happen," I informed her. "And now isn't the time to be thinking about that!"

I pulled out her notebook from my bag, and she began to flip through it. Her smug face said she wasn't over the Dylan and Joey talk.

All the groups should be finished; group Y had the biggest area to booby trap.

"They didn't even get the one grenade," I reminded her.

It won't matter as long as the plan stays on track; the one Cherry has will be enough to stir the interest we need.

"Enough to stir a rebellion, you mean, right?"

She smiled, and handed me the notebook with a page open.Here is the speech you prepared.

"So what if group Y and A don't make it here?"

She shook her head no firmly, it's better if you don't let them inside if they do.

"What why?"

Why? You know why; this is a suicide mission; Joey knows that, Dylan knows that.

"Does Goomba know that?"

Goomba is still 17.

"You just said it was a suicide mission; his age won't matter when he dies."

Goomba isn't going to die.

"Jackson wasn't supposed to die either!"

That doesn't matter now, does it?

"It will matter in a bit when word comes out a guard is dead, and _"

The faint distant sound of sirens entered my eardrum; I jumped up to look out the window.

Goomba's voice screamed through the walkie, "Alice, the five-zero is here!'

I ran into the other room. Goomba wasn't watching the cameras, but rather he was looking out the east window. Two squad cars were at the gate, and Joey was screaming at them while waving his shotgun.

"Get him inside here, Jesus Chryslar!"

Instead of running back down, Goomba grabbed his phone, and dialed Joey's burner number.

"Uh, hello, hey, Alice said get back inside."

We could see Joey on the phone, and then we saw as he unlocked the gate as he told us, "Dylan is here."

"Where is Steven?" I questioned.

Goomba's phone was on speaker so Joey heard me, "The cops got him."

"Fuck!"

"Get back up here, and tell the cops to stay away or this Curtis guard-guy gets it."

Joey hung up, and then yelled at the cops through the gate. He walked away facing the cops with Dylan carrying three backpacks of stuff.

"Go help Dylan," I informed Goomba, but we both went.

Another police cruiser pulled up, and it was followed by a fire truck.

Dylan's cheeks were rose colored, and he was panting hard as he told me,"One of those coppers tackled Steven, he got up, but they tased him."

"Shit. What were you telling them?" I asked Joey.

"I told them we have hostages," Joey responded.

"Did you let them know we would be releasing a statement soon?"

"Yeah, I told him. He wasn't really listening until I said we got hostages."

"I said we got two just like I was supposed to say," Joey clenched his fists.

"Two?" Goomba asked. "Why did he say two? We got one."

Dylan chugged water.

"Oh, Goomba, you ain't know? We got two," Joey informed him.

"Two? Who is the other one?" Goomba asked, but he knew.

Dylan smiled at him, "Goomba, you are." The red was leaving his face.

"No! No! Alice, say it ain't so! I ain't trying to be a hostage!"

I walked close to him, touched his cheek with my left hand, "It is better this way."

Tears rolled down his face, "Fuck no it ain't!"

"I hung up the big white sheet with the owl on it," Joey informed me. Goomba nor I could see him from our vantage point when he did it because he was under the east facing camera.

"What sheet?" Goomba asked.

"Y'all didn't see it?" Joey questioned.

"I did," Dylan said.

"What was it?" Goomba wondered aloud.

"It's an Owl like the one Alice has on her dress there, but I spray painted it onto the sheet."

"The Owl Rebellion," Goomba said with amazement in his words.

Joey patted him on the shoulder, "It is all happening."

Under the giant owl, Joey wrote #OwlRebellions and #FuckBrands which was his own personal slogan, but the Moonlighters adopted it because most brands were major corporations who were ruining the planet.

We all unloaded Dylan's bags, and my burner rang.

"Hello?"

"Mission accomplished," X informed me.

"Great," I said. "How many workers were there?"

"It was just the five as predicted. The place is a mess now, and notes are on the gate, the door, and the place has string, gasoline, propane tanks; I mean stuff is everywhere."

"Good."

"We are moving on to phase two."

"Move beyond it; we are already locked in here."

"No?" X questioned. "There is nothing on the scanner."

"Oh, I can assure you there is, X-man!" Joey yelled over me.

"Damn it! Okay, okay, okay, we will prepare for phase three."

"Get on it."

"We already made the call to 9-11; did group Y make it inside?"

"Negative."

X didn't say anything, but we could all hear how upset he was in the silence.

"This works out better for you, X," Dylan said.

"Yeah, whatever."

"Get moving with the next phase; it is now or never."

X knew, and we all knew that since they wore masks and gloves and drove stolen cars with stolen tags, it would be a while until they were even suspects. The law would think it was us that did it and not X.

"We are on it, good luck."

"You too."

I hung up, and turned to Goomba, "Let's do this video."

"Do you want to clean the blood off your face?"

"I thought I did."

"No, it is still there," Goomba pointed to my forehead.

"Fuck it, Alice, leave it on," Joey said.

"Yeah, you are right. I should have left it all on; move the camera back, I want them to see the blood all over my dress."

The embroidered owl was covered in blood, but most of it was on the bottom of my dress.

Goomba repositioned the tripod, made a few adjustments, and asked if I was ready.

Yes, I nodded.

"Three, two," Goomba said as his hand flashed into a single digit and he pointed at me.

"Good Morning, world…"

CHAPTER 25

Day One, Hour One

None of us had a house phone so the ringing startled us. The antique, brown phone appeared to jump up with each ring.

"What are all those other buttons?" Goomba wondered.

"Pick it up," Joey snapped, but he reached for it.

I grabbed it before he did.

"Uh, hello?"

"This is Sheriff Herbert Jones, who am I speaking with?"

"This is, uh, Alice, Alice Moon, Sheriff."

I covered the mouthpiece and whispered, "It's the sheriff."

"Did they miss the video?" Dylan inquired.

We all looked at Goomba.

It had been an hour since I recorded the message, and Goomba sent it out to local news outlets and the local police. We also sent it out to national media stations, but we assumed they would pick up the story.

"Hello, I know you are on the other end, can you hear me, Alice?"

"Yes, I am here. Did you not get our video?"

"Video? What video?"

"We emailed you a video."

Now I heard the sheriff cover his phone and yell out to the men around him, "did we get a video?"

His voice grew, "Did we get a video in our email?"

"Yes, let me make sure I sent it to you, Sheriff."

I stared at Goomba waiting for confirmation.

"What's his name?"

"Sheriff Herbert Jones."

I was talking to Goomba, but the Sheriff thought I was speaking to him.

"Yes, that is me; I am here. I don't have access to my email right now."

"He doesn't have access to his email right now."

Dylan laughed, "The damn boomer! I swear it. Kentucky elects the dumbest people to office."

"What email should I send it too?" I questioned.

"One second," the sheriff again spoke to the people around him. "She said she can send a video with their demands or what not, but we need a good email. How do we do that?"

There was dead air, and speaking that wasn't understandable, and then a woman got on the other end.

"Hello, yes, can you hear me? This is Carrie Ann. Carr-E Ann Kamper with a K."

"Yes."

"The sheriff doesn't have access to his email right now. That is mostly used for his campaign, but maybe I can help you."

"Okay, well can I email you the video?"

"No, I cannot get an email right now. We are out in the field if I was at my desktop; let me find someone with a computer right here."

"Hello," a new voice spoke into the phone.

"Yes, so I have an email on my phone that you can send it to."

"Okay, what is it?"

"It is Dee Hawkins Sexy, but sexy is spelled s-e-x-x-i, and then the number six and the number nine."

"Sixty-nine?"

"Yes."

"Nice!" Dylan joked.

I wrote it down and handed it to Goomba.

"This isn't an email address; what's the rest of it?"

"What's the rest of it?"

"Oh, that is it."

"So it is DHawkinsSexxi69?"

"Yes."

"She said that's all it is."

"No, what's the rest like at yahoo or at gmail or what?"

"I need to know the rest like is it a yahoo name or gmail email or what?"

"Oh, right so that is at A O L dot com."

"AOL?" Goomba snickered. "It might not even get through on those old ass servers."

Panic began to set in as I wondered about the other plants. If the video didn't get through, who knows what happened at the other plants.

"Did you guys get our notes on the other plants?"

"Uhm, yes, well, we didn't, but the local PD over there did. So you set booty traps in those plants?"

I didn't respond. I couldn't or I might give it away.

"There was owls on those notes just like the owl hanging outside the power plant on the white sheet."

I still didn't respond.

Her voice was cutting, "Hello?"

"So the video is being sent now."

"Okay, well, we need to -"

I hung up the phone.

"What did they say?" Joey asked.

"Nothing. Nobody has seen the video."

"What about the other plants?"

"Yeah, they saw the notes, and now they know it has booty traps."

"Send them the video," Dylan said, but Goomba was.

Joey began to pace, "Maybe we need to take that jabroni outside with a gun to his head so they know we actually have him."

"They know," I stated.

Dylan reminded us, "They have Ted and that other worker guy, Curtis. I am sure they told them everything."

Goomba looked up from his laptop, "It's been sent. Uh, a few of the emails bounced so yeah that isn't good. I've sent it to them again."

I nodded, Joey paced, and Goomba sat down; Dylan walked to the window to stare out at the massive amount of police surrounding us.

"The news is here."

The white van with the channel number on the side was indeed parked behind the police.

"How is a local TV station going to broadcast?" Dylan wondered out loud.

"The station probably has a generator to keep them on air," Goomba said.

"Yeah, but power is out across the city; who is watching?"

"We can," I pointed towards a TV in the corner of the room.

We all moved over towards the older model television. It was a flat screen, but still about 15 years old. Goomba turned it on and flipped for the station so we could watch.

CHAPTER 26

Day One, Hour Two

"We are live outside the power plant that has been taken over by a group with no name as of right now. So if you are wondering why your power is off, it has been shut off by the group inside. One guard is dead, and one member of the gang inside is also dead. So two confirmed dead, and if you are joining us via your phone with our livestream, again, the power is out, so most TVs in the area are out, and an unknown group murdered a guard, and forceable took over this power plant, and then they shut down the power. We spoke with Ted Blake, who was working inside when the attack happened."

The television switched to an interview with Ted Blake. He was still dressed for work, but his glasses were removed and hung from a rope around his neck.

"They came in and shooting and took out our front gate man, Tommy. Tommy got a wife, and I know he wasn't one to try anything stupid. They threatened me too. There was a bunch of them and all of them were holding guns. The leader was a boy in a dress, but there was another hot head, poking his gun around."

"How many of them?" the reporter asked, pulling back the microphone.

"There were four of them, including the one who was shot, a lesbo-lesb-ann."

He added the last word with a long pause after it.

"Did they tell you why they are doing this?"

"No, and there ain't no telling. Bunch of punk ass kids is all I could tell. A boy in a dress, and a girl dressed up as a man, and you can see what good it did 'em. The one is dead, and the rest are in for it."

"So they didn't explain why?"

"Nope, nothing at all. It could have been a Youtube prank gone wrong for all I know."

"How old did you believe they were?"

"The oldest might be 18, but it is really tough to say. They were high school age, I reckon."

"Is there anything else you want to add?"

"The boy in the dress had an owl on his dress, I seen it up close, and then they hung up a big sheet with an owl on it, so I reckon that means something."

"Thank you, Mr. Blake."

"Now isn't the only power plant that has been effected so if you are in the west end of Louisville or the south end, your power doesn't come from this plant as it is mainly the east end and out, but two other power plants were attacked this morning and it is assumed by the same people who local PD here is referring to as the owl gang."

The camera switched to a live shot of the power plant with the words across the bottom of the screen reading, "Owl Gang holding Hostages Inside Power Plant." We could all see the window we were inside of on the screen, and the white sheet with the owl on it blew slowly with the breeze.

"This owl gang also left notes at the other two power plants stating booty traps were set. A close inside source has confirmed those notes contained drawings of owls too. Bomb squads are currently heading to those locations now, but there isn't word on what is exactly happening. Hopefully, things will get resolved and power will return to the area soon. So if you are just joining us, and you are wondering why the power is out, we have your answer."

The camera panned back to the talking reporter.

"A terrorist group labeled as of right as the Owl Gang, has cut power here, placed bombs in other plants, and here they are holding hostages. Reports say that demands have been sent to the LPD police chief and the sheriff here in Bullitt County. Hopefully, power will be back on shortly as the entire city and over a quarter of the state is out of power. We are staying here at the scene. Back to you, Stanley."

"The owl gang? Ain't that some shit?" Joey laughed.

"Well, at least they aren't saying the Moon Gang yet, so they don't know who it is," Dylan said.

Dylan's remark came without eye contact with Joey, and it was the first time I'd seen it. They were in a swinging dick competition, and it was going to be trouble if something wasn't done.

"It's fine," I said. "Let's get the guard feed, and let him make a statement."

"I will go talk to him," Joey said.

"No, I will," Dylan said, and things were escalating even though our whole situation was beyond any level we'd ever seen.

"Dylan you go," I ordered.

"Why me? So Joey can stay in here with you?"

"Why do you care?" Joey barked.

"Knock it off!"

They both gave each other a death stare, but Dylan followed orders like he had all along.

Joey came in close to me, but I didn't respond, and I walked away.

The brown phone rang.

"I got it," Joey said, and he was closer than me, but Dylan was closer than him.

Dylan picked it up before Joey could.

"Hello."

I walked towards them both. Joey was reaching for the phone, but Dylan wouldn't give it to him.

"No, you can speak to her."

Dylan put the receiver on his shoulder, "They want to speak to you, Alice."

I grabbed the phone, "Did they ask for Alice?"

"Yes."

"Then they watched the video."

I took the phone.

"Hello."

"Hi, Alice, Dan Robinson, F.B.I; so we got your video, and we heard all your demands, but don't you think you are asking for a bit much?" Dan held out the last part like clothes to dry.

"We won't budge on our demands."

"Right, but, okay, so, Alice, I am going to be honest here, we are the local team here, and a lot of the stuff you are asking for is national stuff that is done by higher ups."

"Higher ups? What do you mean higher ups?"

"Higher ups, I mean, you said America needs to double the efforts promised in the Paris agreement, and cut coal power completely; I mean come on, who do you think you are?"

"You know who I am; I am Alice. I am a citizen of this planet, and it needs to be saved."

"Right, so Alice, a man is dead. A man who was just making ends meet, working nights -"

I cut him off, "two people are dead. The guard shot our man first!"

"Right, well before anyone gets hurt, can I speak with Curtis?"

"Curtis is fine."

"Can I ask him if he is fine?"

"Bring in the guard."

"Sure, one second."

I put the phone into speaker mode as Dylan brought Curtis into the room. He was blindfolded and ziptied.

"He is here, you can ask him whatever you like."

"Hey, Curtis, Buddy, Dan Robinson, F.B.I, how are they treating you?"

"Uh, okay, I guess. I ain't been hurt, really. I been inside the closet by the -"

"You don't need to tell him where you have been," I informed Curtis.

"Right, so Curtis, we know you need some medicine; your wife informed us of the statin pills you are taking so we are going to get you that. Is there any way I can come and Curtis can come outside?”

“Yeah, I need my pills!” Curtis stated.

“No, we have two hostages, and they will stay inside here with us until our demands are met.”

“Yeah, about those demands,” Agent Robinson paused.

“Take him,” I pointed at Curtis, “back into the other room and let him eat.”

“Alice, your demands aren’t something the local Bullitt County can give you. Moving away from fossil fuels, stopping coal power, sinking all the cruise ships; I mean seriously?”

“The cruise ship industry puts out massive amounts of emissions that aren’t regulated by anyone.”

“Yes, but sinking the cruise ship industry?”

“It’s a play on words, but no, our demands allow for the cruise ships to sail, but only using wind.”

“Right, but we don’t have any jurisdiction over the cruise ships; this is Kentucky! There ain’t an ocean for thousands of miles!”

“Well, what can you help us with?”

“Uh, I can help you resolve this, you kids can come out, let Curtis go before he has a stroke, and we can talk about getting you an attorney.”
“No.”

“Why don’t you come out, and we can get power back on for everyone.”

“Our second hostage's name is Eric Williford. We grabbed him off the street; you can inform his parents that he is fine too.”

“No!” Goomba yelled.

“Can I speak with Eric?”

"Eric is fine, and if he wasn't, why would I tell you he is?"

"Alice, listen, I cannot stop fossil fuels, I cannot stop coal power plants from creating energy so -"

"That's right, you cannot, but we can, and we did. Coal isn't being burned at three power plants right now. We are stopping it."

"You need to give it up, and you can come out here and talk about global warming or whatever it is you want to discuss!"

"No, Mr. Robinson, we will not come out. I will send our other hostage, Eric, to the gate to pick up Curtis' medicine."

"We ain't even got the medicine down here yet!"

"Well, call me back when you do!"

I hung up the phone hard.

"What did they say?" Joey asked.

"Tell us," Dylan begged.

The phone rang. I picked it up.

"What? Do you have the medicine?"

"No, okay Alice, look, those demands are beyond anything that I can get you."

"Who can meet my demands?"

"Which one?"

"All of them."

"I don't think even the President could get you those; he might be able to do some of them," Agent Robinson said.

"If the president can get me some of them, then get him on the phone with me."

I slammed the phone down even harder this time.

"What did he -" Joey asked, but he stopped talking as I put my finger up.

The phone rang for a third time; I picked it up.

"Yes, listen, do not call me back until you can meet one of my demands or you have the medicine. Until then, I have nothing to say. If your men make a move, both hostages die, and we start tossing grenades out the windows at your officers. If you try anything, any move at all, the hostages die gruesome deaths."

"Alice, listen -"

"Gruesome deaths, Robinson. I mean we cut off their nuts and shove them into their mouths. This isn't a game to us. So if you want these hostages to stay alive, stay out of this area. We have cameras everywhere, and we also set up booty traps here too!"

"Yeah, about those, so at the other plant, what is going on?"

"We will tell you how to manuever around the pipe bombs once our demands are met!"

"Alice, we need to-"

I hung up the phone. The group was silent. The phone didn't ring a fourth time.

CHAPTER 27

Day One, Hour Four

"I should go out and stand about twenty feet behind him," Joey suggested. His shirt was off, and he was flexing his muscles.

Curtis' medicine arrived, and Goomba, our alleged other hostage, headed to the gate to pick it up.

"There is no point; we have the other hostage so they won't do anything."

"They might coax Goomba into running away."

Goomba snapped, "Why would I run away? I don't even want to be a hostage!"

Goomba wasn't the issue; the issue was Dylan and Joey were still in a competition.

"It is better that way, Goomba," I assured him. "I will go outside and stand behind him."

"No freaking way!"

"No!"

They agreed on something.

Goomba spoke, "If you go, they might take you out thinking if they cut off the head the snake dies. If we all go, then nobody is here to watch or shoot or whatever the guard. They might snipe us all. I will go alone, but Joey and Dylan can both stand at the door to the building."

"Yeah, that does make sense," Dylan added.

"Okay, but I want to get a look behind the building; I have a feeling that that camera,"Joey pointed at the bottom left monitor, "isn't picking up everything."

"I doubt they will risk it," Dylan said.

"You never know. They've done worse," Joey reminded Dylan.

Dylan nodded. They were agreeing again; perhaps my judgement was wrong.

"Maybe I should go out to that area, and you stay watching Goomba," Dylan said.

Joey shook his head no. "No, I should go."

I needed to shut them up before they went at it again for 10 minutes. "Goomba has the right idea. They will be watching our formation so take guns and look military."

Dylan's face grew a puzzled look, "How do we look military?"

"I don't know!" I barked.

"Just follow my lead!" Joey said, and he pulled a handgun from the lower shorts of his camo cargo shorts.

"Don't point that thing at me," Dylan informed him.

"I didn't. I am looking military, unlike you."

"Me? You don't even have a shirt on; what is this a southend picnic?"

"You two need to knock it off; it isn't the time," Goomba reminded them.

"Don't tell me what to do, Goomba," Joey said.

"No, Goomba is the only one using his head here!" I cut him off.

Go now, before they think we're inept."

Dylan and Joey went to their bags which were in separate corners. Alice's warning was correct. I should have made sure both of them didn't make it here. X or Cash or anyone would have been a better fit.

"Someone needs to check on the generator too."

Dylan yelled out, "I got it."

"No, I got it," Joey snapped back across the room.

They both walked to different parts of the room for no reason. They were dancing with each other.

I needed an answer or the dancing would turn into fighting, and that would lead to a perfect opportunity for the FBI to storm in and kill us all.

"I will watch the monitors so when you get down, spread out, and see if you see anyone snooping around."

They were so eager to leave, they left before Goomba did. Goomba shrugged and rolled his eyes before he walked down the stairs. I followed him but stayed at the top.

"Everything okay, Goomba?"

Stopping three steps down, he shrugged his shoulders again, this time tossing his hands over so they were palms up, and looked at me with his little eyes wide open behind his glasses, "Why'd you have to make me the hostage?"

"It was for your own good; you got a future in this world."

"There is no future in this world."

"Well, if there is, don't you think you will be glad to not be in prison or worse?"

"Didn't I show you that I was committed?" He pleaded.

"Yes, but now isn't the time. I have a plan for all of this, and your plan will be to lead other waves. One wave won't save the world, you know that right?"

"How am I supposed to do that?"

"What do you mean how?"

"Is he coming?" Joey barked from downstairs.

"Calm yourself down; he is coming," Dylan snapped.

"One second!" I yelled down the stairs. "You will figure it out later, Goomba, but if you are locked up in prison or worse, how can you help?"

"Or worse is dead right?" His voice was soft, and it was the first time of the day I felt tears might come on from either one of us.

"It is what it is, but right now, you need to get down there and get the meds. Act scared, timid, you know; you are the hostage."

"I am going to check on the generator," Joey yelled, and he cracked the door. He was itching to get outside.

"If you have everything planned, what are you going to do about them?" Gooma pointed down the stairs at Joey and Dylan.

"It's fine," I lied.

Goomba shook his head, "it isn't fine; they both love you, and both think they are the only one. You should have figured it out before all of this -"

He stopped talking.

"Sorry. I shouldn't have said that."

"Their raging testosterone will not be a problem," I said, but I didn't know. And he was right, I should have handled this before we got to this point.

"The plan is working," I reminded him.

"I believe in you, Nick. I always have. I will be right back," he came in for a hug before he finished, and as he got close he whispered into my ear, "I love you, Alice."

"Good luck, Goomba, get back quick. I love you too."

I did love Goomba. It wasn't the same as how I loved Dylan or thought I loved Joey, but I had a love for him.

Goomba walked down the stairs while Joey and Dylan waited anxiously at the door. I walked back slowly to the camera monitors and watched the exchange. Joey and Dylan did look military in a sense; they both went different directions, and went to the back while Goomba went straight out to the gate.

Goomba talked with a man in a suit for a long time, and then the man handed him a yellow envelope. He took it and waved at the man as he left. He ran back towards the door, and he looked scared which was just how I wanted him to act even though he wasn't acting.

Goomba entered first with Dylan behind him, but Joey walked towards the gate to flip off the police. The hero of the movie syndrome was alive and well in Joey, and I was wondering what I saw in him besides his gorgeous body, but it was mostly that mixed with his devotion to the cause or me. I didn't know which it was yet.

Goomba ran up the stairs, and he was out of breath when he arrived in the room. Dylan came in second.

"Did you see what the asshole did? He flicked off the cops!"

"What? No?" Goomba said while gasping for air.

"Yes, I saw it," I said.

Joey arrived a minute later.

"What in the hell was that about?" Dylan asked.

"What?"

"You know what! You ran back out there to flick off the police!"

"Yeah I did! And the TV cameras!" Joey yelled.

"Why? This isn't about you getting views with your shirt off, Jesus, fuck, dude," Dylan was pissed.

"Knock it off!" Goomba said.

It would take more than that to end it.

"Joey, you need to check on the generator; Dylan, you need to check on the guard. He will need his medicine. Goomba, what's in the envelope?"

"I did it is good," Joey answered as he unfolded his shirt to put it on.

"Check it again," I said firmly.

"Fucking Showbiz Pizza over here," Dylan said.

"Showbiz? What does that even mean?"

"Hey, cut it out!" I yelled, and I stood between them.

"The guy said my mom wants me to call her," Goomba said.

"Do they know who you are?"

"Yes, you told them."

"I mean like your mom contacted them, or they contacted her and she said that?"

"Yes. They said they put a phone in here too."

Goomba opened the envelope; he poured out the contents. There were two phones both older models, a list of all the demands from the video listed out, and a pill bottle with Curtis' name on it.

"Those phones are listening devices; we need to drop them in water," Joey said.

"Yeah, I agree," I added. "They know we have a phone; go get rid of them."

Joey grabbed the phones, and he ran towards the bathroom; Dylan walked towards the guard with his medication, and I sat down wondering what would happen next.

CHAPTER 28

Night One

Despite paranoia from everyone, we made it through the first night without an attack. We all assumed a Ruby Ridge type of ordeal would happen, but we were grateful it wasn't on the first night. And I was hoping it would be avoided all together, but the first night would have been detrimental to our mission.

Keeping Dylan and Joey away from each other was an issue; both of them had a lot of hormones coursing through them. Separating them was the key so they were positioned at opposite ends of the second floor; each was given a window and made to feel important.

We agreed to release the bodies to the police. Goomba drove the car to the gate, left the keys inside the ignition with the car running, and he bounced back to the building. Joey and Dylan walked around the building again.

"One person was yelling at me; they were like come here, come here," Goomba informed me when he got back.

They were testing him, or testing if he was a real hostage.

"I yelled at them; I have to get back or they will kill Curtis."

"Then what?"

"I don't know; I ran back."

I told Dan Robinson that Jackson was a hostage too. We'd picked Jackson up when we grabbed Goomba. It didn't matter if he believed me, maybe Jackson's mom would.

The stress levels dropped an ounce, but we were still on high alert. My mind was twisted and foggy like I'd stayed up all night. It was hard to focus on anything.

Joey cooked the fresh meat we had; there was no point in saving it. We had the canned goods for saving. We'd brought in tons of food, but it wouldn't last long if we ate large helpings. Curtis ate the most, but I made sure he stayed away from everyone else.

Joey duct taped his hands behind his back, and Curtis bitched about it, but it had to be done.

"If you don't give us any trouble, we can have you sleep with them in front of you tomorrow night."

Curtis went on and on about some new bed he'd just bought, and how his back was bad, but we couldn't risk him fleeing.

The police presence outside appeared miles deep. We'd spot snipers up in the trees, and dial out to tell Dan Robinson he better get them down. They'd go down, but an hour or two later, someone would spot another one, and we'd start it all over.

Contacting Dan Robinson was easy, we didn't have to dial out. All we had to do was pick up the phone, and it would start ringing. Who knows how the feds got that to work, but it did.

"They can probably listen to us from that TV!" Joey said, but I wasn't worried about it.

"Any speaker is a microphone."

"They'd have to access it, and that TV isn't a smart TV," Goomba said.

"What about on your laptop?" Joey pointed at Goomba's laptop which had a red case with Super Mario on it.

"It isn't even opened," Goomba answered.

"Yeah, but what about when it is?"

"They have devices they can aim at us to hear us," Dylan said.

And it was shortly after that I separated them.

Joey was in a hallway by a woman's bathroom, and he kept a chair by the blinds closed except for a small slint so he could see out. He had two handguns, both of them at his feet, a loaded sawed off shotgun on the wall, and a sniper's rifle of sorts that he used to hunt. He was on edge, but when we were alone, he calmed his nerves a bit.

"We are actually doing this; it's kinda fun, ain't it?" His shirt was off, and he'd been doing pushups.

It wasn't fun. Not even a little bit.

"Not really."

"You know what I mean, Alice; you still got a little blood on your face."

He rubbed his thumb across my forehead, but the dried blood didn't budge. He told me so, and then he licked his thumb and tried again.

"It's okay," I pulled my head back.

"I gotta go get some sleep. You will be okay staying up for a bit?"

"Yeah, you ain't gonna stay with me?"

Normally, Joey was tough as nails, and he wouldn't ask for any type of sympathy, but he pulled that card as soon as I tried to leave him. "You can stay for a bit, right?"

He reached out to touch my arm, and held my hand.

"Joey, I gotta go; I will be back, okay?"

"Are you going to sleep with Dylan?"

"No. I am going to sleep by myself. Dylan has to watch out of the south where the cameras cannot see."

"Okay, why don't you go check in with him, and then come back and see me, huh?"

"I might."

I dropped his hand, and left the room not turning back to look at him.

Dylan wasn't as locked and loaded, but he did have one of the sawed off shotguns and a revolver that belonged to his grandfather.

"Hey," he said softly as soon as I walked into the room.

Dylan was sharper than Joey, and he was starting to figure things out, but now wasn't the time. He was in a break room; it had a small round table, a microwave, and a sink. The window was behind him, and he also had the blinds down except for one.

"Hey," I responded just as softly. "You know, Joey is looking out the north window, Goomba has the camera's looking east and west. How is the south window?"

"Not shit but a squirrel and a racoon. No snipers, no movement."

"You gonna stay down here with me for a bit?" He reached out and grabbed my hand.

"You got dried dirt or muck on your forehead."

"It's blood. Jackson's blood."

My eyes felt warm in the corners, but I pressed the tears back until I noticed his eyes were tearing up.

One small drop fell out of my eye and down my left cheek.

"If I woulda been here, maybe that wouldn't have happened!"

"Why didn't you have me here instead of J-" He stopped himself.

"If it was you instead of Jackson, then you'd be dead."

"Instead of Joey?"

"You had to lead the other mission; I didn't think you'd even -"

"You didn't think I'd make it back did you?"

"No, I didn't say that."

"Yeah, but did you plan it?"

"It was in my plans wasn't it?"

"I don't know about Steven; he was nervous, and I didn't think he even wanted to make it. It was like he wanted to get caught."

"It's okay; we know even some of the Moon Gang would try to stop us."

"I like the owl on your dress," Dylan was more intuitive than Joey and Goomba.

"Thanks. The owl can be a sign of a rebellion."

"I know just like you want to start, right?"

"If we can; I mean, what else are we risking our lives for, right?"

Dylan brought his face in to kiss me, but I moved mine backwards.

"It's not the time, Dylan. We gotta stay focused on the task."

"I'm sorry; you are just so beautiful, Alice."

"It isn't the time, okay?"

"One kiss? We cannot do one kiss?"

"How is the generator?"

"Joey checked it and said it was good."

"Did you check it?"

"No, should I?"

"No. If it goes out, it goes out."

"Half the power is out across the state so we can't be beggars now."

"It's not half the state."

His head moved in closer, but not to kiss me. He just moved it in closer to talk.

"You knew I would make it here, right?"

"Yes."

I was lying, and I couldn't look at him even though his eyes were on top of mine.

His smell returned to me, and it turned me on so I pushed him away and stood up.

"I am glad you made it inside, but it was always the plan. We needed Steven, and it would have been nice to have some of the others. Now we are going to rotate shifts looking out the windows and watching the cameras. I am going to get some sleep, and I will come check on you in a bit."

"I don't need you to check on me; I will watch the window all night."

"You will have to sleep sometime, Dylan."

"I will sleep tomorrow when the sun is out, and we have a better view. Go get some rest; I am awake and ready."

I walked towards the door because I couldn't look back at him.

"We are doing the right thing even though Jackson died."

I turned around with my feet in the doorway, "Yeah, I hope so because I am really starting to question everything."

"This was our only option; we had no other choice."

"I hope so."

"I'm going to go check on Goomba and get some rest."

"Alice, I love you."

"Would you be here if you didn't love me?"

"I am here because I do."

The movement sank a few levels, and my stomach turned.

Both of these young men were here because they thought they loved me. They were infatuated with me, and it led them on this wild mission that might get them killed. Did they care about the future of the world or did they care about me? The answer to that question matterered. It mattered a lot.

"I love you too, Dylan. Thank you, thank you for coming here."

"We are going to change the world."

"I hope so."

CHAPTER 29

Day Two

When the distant sun crept up in the corner of the eastern window signaling we'd made it through the first night, we collectively breathed a sigh of relief. Every sound was an FBI ambush, and every time I closed my eyes, I saw a helicopter outside the window so I didn't sleep much. I really felt in my gut that the FBI would bumrush the building around five. When five came and went, I finally got some sleep. The reasoning for the five am time was based on nothing but my own gut. It was a thrill to be wrong.

As daylight fell upon us, and the birds began to sing outside the windows, Curtis yelled about needing to use the restroom. Joey took care of that, and I went to check on Goomba. He was asleep with his head resting on his hand which was held up by his elbow.

"I'm not asleep," He informed me with a drool running down his chin, and his eyes half shut.

"I can see you aren't," I responded. "Any action on the cameras last night?"

"A few racoons, huh?"

"Coffee?"

"All they have is Folgers, and Folgers taste like butt."

"Oh, so you like it?" It was an attempt to keep things light.

Goomba smiled and pointed at his cup, "I already had some."

"I will get you another cup of butt."

I took his cup, and the phone rang. It startled both of us.

"Hello?"

"Good morning, uh, Alice, so what do you say? You can let Curtis go, and we will get y'all some flapjacks with syrup."

"Flapjacks, huh? What about sausage?"

"We can do bacon and whatever else you need; you know Janey, Curtis' wife was here all night. She slept in a patrol car."

"We got some room for her in here."

"Alice, can we stop this? Eric's mom is coming down here, and she wants to see her boy. I am hoping you will let Eric, Goomba, that's what you call him, right?"

"Uh-huh."

"We are hoping you let Goomba come talk to his mom when she gets here; can we do that?"

"You guys really want him to run off don't you?"

"Oh no, Alice."

"Yeah, you figure if he escapes, then all you got is old Curtis in here, and you guys will come flying in like Waco, Texas, right?"

"Waco, Texas?"

"Or like you did to Breonna Taylor, huh?"

"Alice, you know the hospitals don't have power. People are going to die."

"The hospitals should have all the solar panels they need. We stole them from Churchill Downs."

I was admitting to another crime, but at this point it didn't matter.

"They are trying to get them hooked up before the generators die. I can see your generator is working; how does that make you feel?"

"How does what make me feel?"

"How do you feel being one of the one percent of people in the area to have power right now."

"How are the bomb squads doing at the other plants?"

"Alice, you need to tell us what kinda bombs; are they pipe bombs? We found a few things that look like pipe bombs."

Silence. I'd break if I spoke.

"Alice, we got your mother coming down here too. She was here last night; how do you think she feels?"

Dan Robinson was testing me. Silence. I couldn't show weakness.

"She will be here shortly with flapjacks and bacon and sausage. Why don't I call you back when she is here."

"She will understand why I am doing this."

"Why are you doing this, Alice?"

"You have our list of demands."

"Is that your list, or is that a list you made all together? Did Dylan help or did Joey help?"

Silence.

Dan Robinson was trying another test, but he could only try this one because he knew something. He either had ears inside the building, or he was speaking with someone from the Moon

Gang. Both were equally troublesome. We'd need to start writing things down.

Silence.

"Can Mrs. Williford at least speak with Eric?"

"Yes, call me back when she is here."

"Great, so Alice, what is -"

"You have our list of demands; Call me back when Goomba's mom is here."

I hung up the phone.

"My mom is coming?" Goomba asked.

"Yeah, she will be here shortly."

My mind was exhausted, and it was only the start of day two. The coffee helped, but it also kicked in paranoid thinking.

The call from Goomba's mom arrived at just before 7:30. I let him talk to her, and stayed away checking in on Joey and Dylan. Joey was wired, but not from coffee. He'd drunk it all night, but he was amped up full of adrenaline.

"There's a lot of movement out there," Joey told me while glancing through binoculars.

"More than yesterday?"

"Yep. They are planning something for sure."

"Keep your eyes open; I will be back."

Dylan wasn't as frantic, but his alarm was up too.

"The SWAT team is here."

"Already?" I asked.

"It might just be protocol, but they are here. They showed up around five."

He handed me his binoculars, and pointed in a direction.

"Damn."

I walked back into the room with Goomba in it, and asked if he was done. He nodded so I hung up the phone.

"What's up?"

"SWAT is here."

"Shit."

He handed me the receiver so I let go of the hook; the phone rang.

Dan Robinson was on the line. "Hello, did something happen, Eric and his mother were cut off."

"No, that is all the time he has. Why is the SWAT here, Dan?"

"The SWAT? That is just protocol."

"Okay, well I want them backed up."

"Excuse me?"

"You heard me, Dan; have them back up out of my sight."

I wanted to add, "or we start killing hostages," but it was better not to.

"I guess I can see what I can do, is that a new demand?"

"No, but it needs to happen."

"If it happens can we get power going for the people?"

"No."

"Okay, so no power for the people of Louisville, huh?"

"Move the SWAT back."

"Okay, I will see what I can do."

I hung up, and looked at Goomba. I picked up a pen and wrote down, "They are listening to us."

He mouthed, "I know."

I took the paper into Joey's room and showed him; he nodded.

"See if Goomba can find some notebooks."

"Yeah, he needs to since he is our hostage!"

Goomba found some notebooks, and I took one to Dylan with my note. He wrote down, "yeah, I figured."

We watched as the SWAT truck backed away, and parked just out of our vision.

"We can see them coming better now," I wrote down, and Dylan nodded.

It was going to be a long day.

CHAPTER 30

Day Seven, One Week

According to Joey the SWAT is preparing to rush us; he's been saying that since day two, but his concern grows with each passing day. His alarm is full tilt. All he can think about in his room, looking out the window, is an impending attack. To save his sanity, I assigned him to work on the generator while Goomba took over watch duty.

The generator ran out of gas despite all the backup fuel, but Joey ciphered gas from a few trucks, and we are back in business for two more days. The irony of having electricity while cutting it off for millions of people is not lost on anyone. He also positioned the work trucks as another line of defense for us.

We can suffer in the god-awful heat like everyone else, I informed Joey before he stole the rest of the gas. The heat is best met with no clothes so the law is getting glimpses of us in underwear as we maneuver through a surprise heat wave inside a building built to hold in the heat.

It isn't quite a million without power, but we couldn't have picked a better time to get a point across. The whole planet will be hotter than this if emissions aren't lowered yesterday. We all understand the mission.

Goomba informed me that the power plant supplying the east end has been nearly cleared entirely by the bomb squad. They didn't find any bombs, but they've been scouring it like hunting roaches.

We are starting to get the attention of the rest of the country now too. We were a trending topic on social media, and gaining quite the online presence. Most of it is hate, and I cannot blame the Louisvillians in the dark; this heat wave is unmerciful. It's a good thing we didn't do this for fame or love. We were infamous and hated.

We've all watched enough local news to know we are hated, but Goomba tunes into everything else too. He is armed with three hacked cell phones, and a charger that runs on solar power. Cable news is the worst. Nightly, they drag us through the mud like we are running for office on the opposite side of their agenda. Both sides of the political lines are dumping tar and feathers on our names nightly. The zombies watching all agree that we should be yanked from this building and hung in the nearest tree.

Joey takes it the hardest. He seems to think we are already on death row. We might be, but this is far from over.

"Don't worry about it; it's cable news! The only people watching cable news are zombie boomers. They hate us just for being young. They knew about this mess, and they didn't do shit about it."

He agrees with me, but he's on edge.

Last night a white conservative (is there any other kind?) pundit with his hair slicked back attacked our families. His rant to end his "news" program rallied the base which sadly is a big majority of those that live in Kentucky. The rant hit social media titled as "The Inmates Have Taken Over the Power," and it brought in millions of views live and even more post broadcast.

"Millions are without power during this heat wave in Louis-Ville, Kentucky because of the actions of Nick Moon and his Moon Gang. Last week these thugs rushed the power plant while armed, murdering one guard, holding others hostage while cutting the electricity to millions of properties. Now, Kentucky is in a major heat wave, and without power, hundreds if not thousands will die. Why? Well, the list of demands sounds like a liberal commercial for a new green deal. Their demands include ending coal power, sinking the cruise ships industry, ending fossil fuel dependency, and more. And while the city of LouE-Ville, is without power, these hoodlums have a working generator and they are enjoying beverages with ice during this heat wave.

Now in any other situation, the President would send in the national guard and remove these alphabet gangsters, but not our President, and for all we know, he is likely a supporter of this agenda.

Now reports are coming out that Nick Moon is a homosexual, and as you know, we don't hate homosexuals, but we know it is a disease of the mind. Nick Moon is also allegedly a transgender, and again, this is a disease of the mind. Nick Moon is insane, crazy, and now he controls the button of power for millions of folks in Kentucky. This is another reason the President won't act; he doesn't want to offend the voters in the alphabet community. These LGBTQ and radical liberals are at it again, but shutting down the power is a new low. Maybe, just maybe, these folks need their houses burned to the ground, and then Nick Moon and his heathen gang followers might feel the heat too. Bring the heat to the families of these thugs!

The thugs have ice, and the good, hard working folks of Looey-ville can't even get dressed in the morning until the sun comes up. Don't you think if this transexual's mom's house was burnt to the ground, they might think twice about messing with the power grid? Millions are without power, those who need prescriptions are depending on the few pharmacies with generators, and why? So the Democrats can pass a new green deal? It is beyond outrageous.

If this transexual's mom's house was burnt to the ground, don't you think he would think twice about messing with the power grid? Millions are without AC during the biggest heat wave in fifty years and for what? So the Democrats can get a new green deal? No, his house needs to be destroyed, and notice I said he, right? That is because Nick Moon is a male; he was born a male, and his license says he is a male. He can put on a dress, but it is still basic science that he is a male. We need to end the gay agenda in this country!"

There is no way for me to contact Mom, but I hope she stays safe with this type of rhetoric happening. I cannot speak with her, but news reporters found her, and Goomba showed me the clip.

It was local channel three, and Mom was wearing her work clothes. Heat jumped to the side of my eyes as I watched her.

"Mrs. Moon, what do you have to say to your son, Nick?"

"I would tell him that I love him, and - "
Mom was crying so hard she couldn't finish the sentence.

The reporter didn't wait, "Would you tell your son to stand down? Millions of people don't have power, and this heat wave is relentless. People are dying without access to power. Can you ask your son to surrender?"

Mom removed the kleenex from her face and calmed herself with a big swallow. She shook her head back and forth and closed her eyes before she spoke.

"No. No, I would tell Nick to keep fighting. Nick isn't doing this because he is a bad person; Nick is doing this because he is a good one. He is fighting for all of us. You, me, everyone. Nickie, if you see this, I love you, and keep fighting!"

"Your son might be killed if the national guard rushes the building."

"He might; you are right. Nick is willing to die to save the planet, and I couldn't be more proud of him. Nickie, I love you."

"Your mom is awesome," Goomba said.

She was, and that meant our message was getting out. It wasn't broadcast on the news, but my video of demands was making the rounds on social. The views were piling up, and luckily, Mom watched it. She understands it too.

Most of Kentucky hated us, but not everyone. The heat was making it easier though.

Goomba was getting emails, and reading comments on social media to keep us informed. The supporters weren't snowballing into a movement, but they were visible. Goomba gave us daily reports from both sides.

Despite these daily updates from Goomba, he was falling apart. He would hold his composure during the day, but at night, he would bawl his eyes out. The burden of killing the guard wore on him, and Jackson's death was cutting at him too. Goomba loved Jackson just like we all did. He wasn't supposed to die; nobody was supposed to die for our mission. We understood that some might, but none of us thought it would really happen.

Joey rigged the camera's up to two of the truck batteries so we can still have eyes on the gate and the far north entrance. It was one of Jackson's ideas, and Joey walked around with a sense of accomplishment when he got it all running. He thanked Jackson a million times; shit, we all did. Jackson would have been one helluva mechanic.

Curtis became the real surprise. He was actually a cool guy for a boomer. Goomba chats with him the most. He asked us about why we were doing this, and when we told him, he shook his head and cussed. He works at a coal plant so he might be the type of person who will never believe in the climate crisis, but he's slowly understanding it.

Curtis also said we could burn a small amount of coal and bypass the generator to get power. We aren't burning any coal, and we told him this. Goomba and Dylan have been reading him so many scientific facts on the climate crisis that he might break. I wouldn't bet on it though.

The hormones seem to be the biggest battle, but as long as Dylan and Joey stay apart, the mood is calm. They both believe in the fight, but I wish I knew if they loved me more or the mission more. It's both, but I wish I knew what percentage. If I had to guess I'd say Joey is 60-40; the 60% being the mission, but Dylan is the opposite; Dylan is 60-70% here just for me.

Dylan has written me a letter every night professing his love for me. I read his notes, and I listen to him, but it is not where I wanted to be seven days into the mission. Time will tell what happens.

CHAPTER 31

The **MOON** Gang, Dextromethorphan, Collapse, Climate Crisis, Tupac, LGBTQ, the Highlands, **Gay Fight Club,** Crossdressing Teenage Love Affair, **MOONlighters,** Machiavelli, Alice Einstein, SAVE the World, **Global Warming,** Masquerading, Transgendered, Robo-Tripping, **Owl Rebellion**

Robo-tripping is the act of getting high by drinking a lot of over-the-counter Robitussin, which contains a drug called Dextromethorphan, which has effects similar to psychedelic mushrooms.

Joey spotted them first; the first supporters of our cause lined up with picket signs outside the police perimeter. It began with a man and woman only, but the numbers grew each day so by day nine it was a large chunk of folks we could see through the binoculars. As the tenth day hit, Dylan noticed some familiar faces among the bunch. X and Rex were yelling at the cops and wearing shirts with owls across the chest.

It was happening. The movement was becoming real. Our idea of fluttering our butterfly wings to start a tsunami had wind. It was becoming a real thing because of a piece published in the

New Yorker, or at least, that is what we attributed it too.

And it was becoming real because of a rush piece published in the New Yorker, or at least, that is what we attributed it too. The piece written by New Yorker writer Kathryn Schulz didn't contain all facts but it raised awareness of our movement.

It was the first positive message put out by the press, and it wasn't fuel to our flame because our fire was extinguishing; it was the spark to start a real fire as ours extinguished.

"How an Electric Group of Teenagers Brought Darkness to Kentucky"

By

Kathryn S.

Tuesday June 22nd

It was a soft, watercolor June summer morning outside of Louisville, Kentucky when a pale white Lexus holding teenagers Nick Moon, Joey Fryar, Eric "Goomba" Williford, and Amber "Jackson" Carter pulled into the Meade Road power plant one hour before the night shift would clock out. The crickets were awake, chirping as guard Thomas "Tommy" Gonterman informed the group of kids that they couldn't do a u-turn on the other side of the locked gate.

What happened next is up to who you speak with; most who know Tommy say he does carry a weapon on him at all times, even at work at the power plant where it is illegal. Tommy is a gun-toting patriot, who considers himself an armed "good guy" in case a mass shooting pops off.

"Tommy was defending the power plant; he knew troublemakers when he saw them," Tommy's sister Darlene informed me when I spoke with her at a Denny's on Dixie Highway in Louisville, Kentucky.

"They were armed bandits, and look at the trouble they caused! Tommy knew that and he tried to stop them. We haven't had power in six days!"

It is now day eight, and power is still off for most of Jefferson County.

Tommy was shot by the troublemakers, but only after he executed his good guy with a gun fantasy. Tommy fatally shot Amber "Jackson" Carter. Jackson was only 17 years young; a tomboy who dressed like a male, worked on cars, and wanted to become a car mechanic.

The facts in the invasion are limited to only that Tommy is dead and Jackson is dead. The rest is a puzzling mystery local law enforcement is trying to solve in the dark.

Tommy's family claims the 63 year old night shift worker was protecting his work. The story has been repeated on local news and in the local paper, but the city is mostly in the dark about the real story.

Tommy's co-worker, Ted Blake, tells a different story. Blake was on duty working the night shift with Tommy, when he heard gunfire. Blake claims he came outside and Jackson was already dead, but Tommy was claiming it was an accidental unloading of his weapon that caused the death.

"Wrong spot, wrong time," I quoted Blake.

A tall southern man, Blake spoke with me three times, once standing outside his house as his wife cooled the dogs down using the car's air conditioning.

"Tommy was still alive after this; they put him into the trunk, and the short little guy who they are saying is a hostage, he shot Tommy when he was in the trunk. That's an odd thing for a hostage to do. They put Tommy in the trunk, and he stole one of their shotguns, but he didn't have any bullets. They smashed his head in, but the little guy with the dark hair and the beady eyes, he opened the trunk, stuck a sawed off shotgun in there and shot Tommy point blank."

A giant white sheet with an enormous black owl was hung from outside the facilities.

It only got weirder from this point.

The group of teenagers entered the building, holding Ted at gunpoint, and forced the power to be cut.

"They had guns on me, and I took 'em to Curtis who is still inside. They said shut it off!" Ted makes a gun with his pointer and middle finger, his thumb raised, and he puts it down below his belt. "They were pointing handguns at his manhood when they told him. He jumped up and they went to turn the power off. That's when the leader tells me, I am free to go. I gotta get out before they lock the gate."

The leader of the gang was Nick Moon aka Alice Moon. (We will get into the AKA later; I told you it gets weird.)

"He was the leader. He was wearing a blue and white dress, and he didn't have a weapon that I saw, but was the leader. The other boy flying the gun all over the place was tough, but he was taking orders from the male in the dress. He was barking orders, and they all followed him."

Heath Ledger playing the Joker, dressed as a nurse in a dress comes to mind. The sinister Joker dances as bombs explode around him; Nick Moon, Kentucky's new Joker.

"He was a good kid, always helping his mom out. He used to walk around the neighborhood picking up trash with a stick and trash bag," one neighbor told us.

Another told me, "When my husband had his heart attack he came over and cut our grass. He never asked for money, and his momma said it was all they could do to help."

The scale of how nefarious Nick Moon and Moon Gang is, seems to be a sliding scale depending on who you ask. We've seen too often how mass shooters are labeled as good folks by their teachers and parents, and the fact of two people being dead and close to 500,000 without power isn't forgotten. It is a massive emergency for the state of Kentucky. Nick Moon appears to be on this same sliding scale.

In true Joker Comicbook fashion, earlier in the morning of June 22nd, Nick and his Moon Gang, entered two other power plants, wrecking havoc while wearing face masks of the Kardashians and Jenners. They sabotaged the plants, shut the power down, and then set booty traps around the premises before fleeing. Notes were left behind along with instructions to make pipe bombs. All the notes were inscribed with an owl at the top. The local bombsquad and FBI units are almost done sweeping the two buildings, but no bombs have been found yet.

The power is slowly being turned back on, but the fear of a bomb exploding remains.

So who is the Moon Gang and why did they shut off power to nearly 500,000 Kentuckians?

The Moon Gang consists primarily of high school teenagers who gather at Nick Moon's mother's house every Thursday night while Pamela Moon works the graveyard shift. The parties were well-known throughout Nick's high school, but only the outcasts attended.

One of the regular guests was senior football player, Joey Fryar. I spoke with his former girlfriend, Brooke Ann Stevens about the parties:

"They were crossdressing parties; Joey would wear a skirt and call himself Wanda, but I only heard about it after it happened from a guy who went to the parties but got out of there when they started planning to take out the electricity."

Stevens said the party was full of homosexuals.

"They were mostly gay kids who couldn't hang out at the other parties because they were gay, obviously, and we didn't want crossdressing at our parties."

When asked if Joey, a male she dated was gay, "No, I don't think Joey was gay, but I don't know. I heard they had orgies and stuff at these parties, but I never went. They would all dress up like women, it was weird. They also robo-tripped, which is like for freshmen who cannot score any weed."

The masquerading parties included robo-tripping. Robo-tripping is the act of getting high by drinking a lot of over-the-counter Robitussin, which contains a drug called Dextromethorphan, which has effects similar to psychedelic mushrooms.

Clark, a former member of the Moon Gang, who would like to keep his last name and identity hidden, attended these Thursday night shindigs.

"Alice, I mean, Nick, would open the meetings by reading a poem or lyrics from Tupac, and then she, I mean he, would say "Welcome to the gay Fight Club." Everyone would laugh, but nobody was fighting. It was just supposed to be a safe place for everyone to act how they wanted. Nick would dress up as Alice, and Joey would sometimes be Wanda. Not everyone dressed up, but some did and it was fine. Not everyone was gay either which should be noted."

When asked about the Robo-tripping, Clark said, "We didn't do it every time, but if it was your first time, you had to do it. I think that's why Alice said welcome to Fight Club. You know how in Fight Club if it's your first time, you gotta fight, well, if it is your first time, you gotta trip."

Clark filled me in on why Nick would dress up as Alice.

"She wanted to be our Alice in Wonderland. Alice's trip into Wonderland represents how kids struggle to survive in the confusing world of adults. Alice has to overcome her open-mindedness that all kids have, and conform a certain way if she wants to understand what it means to live in the adult world. Nick, or Alice, well, he didn't want us to conform that way. Why should we change to fit in? That was her whole message."

The Thursday night parties lasted all night under the moonlight behind the Moon house, a rented one bedroom with an attic converted into a second floor. Tupac poems were read, Einstein's theories were passed around, and they all collectively read The Prince by Machiavelli. It was a created safe haven for anyone to attend and feel safe.

The nights tore into the mornings, and often the discussion switched into what Clark described as, "the incoming collapse of society."

"Alice had a fascination for end times. She searched out the topic, like she was on reddit but only read the Collapse sub. She was ate up the end of the world."

Nick was Alice every Thursday, but Clark didn't know if Nick wanted to always become Alice.

"I don't think he wanted to transition into a woman. Maybe, but he never said that. When he dressed as a woman, he was Alice, but when he wasn't dressed up, he was Nick. We all went with it."

Nick didn't just dress up Thursdays, he also dressed as a female sometimes at school.

"No one really knew how to act when he showed up in the dress. Some of the people that knew him, like the Moonlighters or whatever, they called him Alice when he wore a dress," Brooke Ann Stevens told me. "It was weird, like maybe he is bi-polar, but I don't think kids were overly mean to him. He owned his outfits and sh*t; he carried on like nothing changed, and it was us who had to change. I think that was why some of the other boys didn't like him."

Nick was a quiet kid; described as "popular but not really." A known face, but nobody really knew him. His homeroom teacher, Patty O'neal describes Nick as inscrutable. Mrs. O'neal only spoke with me in person because she had no way to charge her cellular phone with the power out. Her phone had been dead since day one of the blackout.

"I think he knows he is smarter than most of his classmates, but he fits in because he is really smart. When he was a freshman I asked him what he wanted to be when he grew up, and he didn't respond right away. He thought about it, he paused, and then he replied, 'rich, I guess would be nice," but then he shook his head, like he knew he had said the wrong thing. He said, 'Being rich seems nice, but I guess as long as my mom and I have enough, I don't need to be rich. I could see myself helping the community as a social worker.'"

"That really stuck with me, because he was serious, it was like he took the question to heart. What did he want to be? He wanted to be rich, but he knew maybe he didn't too. His thoughts immediately went to helping people after that. Nick is unique, but he is a good kid. He slept in class, and he got in trouble for that, but he aced the tests so what can the teachers do if the kid is getting all As?"

Nick was suspended for sleeping in class, but his report card clearly showed an A+ student.

When asked about his crossdressing Mrs. O'neal said, "it kinda grew into a thing with the teachers because he was doing it on casual Fridays and spirit days at first so we would guess if he was going to do it. It was fun for some of us, but for others they didn't like it at all. Some of the staff called him names, queer and fag or liberal, and they really thought it was the end of the world."

Mrs. O'Neal didn't have any knowledge about the Thursday night parties. "Perhaps that is why he was sleeping in class."

The parties grew in size, but nobody ever tried to stop them. It is unknown if Pamela Moon knew about the parties happening while she was working, but most assumed she didn't. Pamela Moon was asked about her son last week by a local news station, and instead of telling her son to stand down, she told her son to keep fighting.

"I couldn't believe it, here we have close to a million without power including herself, and she is telling her son to keep fighting. Keep fighting? She is just as crazy as her boy," Tommy's sister Darlene told me while eating at Denny's, and the waitress waiting on us felt the same way, "We are only open cause we got the generator up and running now. Thousands of businesses are shut down. The court house is shut down, traffic lights are out, the airport is down. How crazy is that? And the man doing it is getting moral support from his mother? These damn liberals are insane."

Darlene informs us both this is happening because, "they won't let God in the schools."

The airport is out of power for the most part, but plans on having flights returned this week are on the menu for the Governor. The bigger ordeal was the hospitals going dark. Hospitals all have battery backups and generators for the most vulnerable, but the first crime by the Moon Gang really showed how this ordeal is stranger than fiction.

"They stole solar panels from around the state, and somehow carried them to the top of two hospitals. And I don't mean a few, I mean a lot of solar panels. Those things are heavy, but they did it."

The Moon Gang stole solar panels and placed them on top of the hospitals, but didn't install them. In the video sent to the FBI and local police and press, this information was supplied, but the panels are not hooked up and no plans have been made to install the stolen property. The hospitals are still using generators as the Governor has issued a state of emergency.

"When I heard that, I knew it was the same guy who cut my grass. He isn't a bad kid; he is just confused and made a terrible mistake," Nick's neighbor informed me.

The total number of Moonlighters is close to thirty. Most were in high school, and all of them had some sort of connection to the Highlands, a portion of Louisville known as a 'lively area full of nightlife,' where the Moon house was located.

Although not all of the members were homosexual, the majority dressed in drag, whether it was boys wearing skirts or dresses like Alice or females dressed as men. Brooke Ann and her friend Kara Long only recently learned of the events, but they had heard conflicting reports throughout the school year.

"We heard about the Robitussin and beer drinking at Nick's house, but we didn't know what was going on exactly. Some kids would say they were fags or whatever, but not in a mean way," Kara Long informed me. "They weren't very popular, but everyone knows everyone. I knew Joey was going before Brooke knew, but she does have a picture of him in drag as "Wanda.""

Brooke went on to talk about the parties, "It was like people Joey made fun of, and I think they brainwashed him because he wasn't gay before. They were dressed as women, drinking a lot of liquor, and reading poetry. It sounded pretty lame."

The parties started in early March, but they continued until the night before they ambushed the power plants and took down the power grid. The FBI is currently interviewing anyone with knowledge of the Moon Gang, and it appears a few of the Moonlighters have been brought in for multiple interviews.

One mistake the Moon Gang made was sending out a video with

their demands in it to a police force and sheriff's office who didn't have power. The five minute video of Nick Moon standing inside the power plant, blood still visible on his dress and face, as he makes demands to return the power. The video is now trending online, and has been for several days. Nick, who calls himself Alice, lays out the facts and speaks with a knowledge of the climate crisis that comes off as grandiloquent to the locals in Kentucky.

The extravagant demands are laid out by Alice, but later added as bullet points over the image of an owl. The same owl on the giant sheet hanging outside the power plant. In laying out the facts, Alice quotes Al Gore from twenty years ago, and Jimmy Carter from almost fifty years ago, but he also adds in recent quotes from scientists, but mainly hangs his hat on the fact that "99% of all scientists agree that this is a real event," which he says three times.

Alice continues, "The richest rich are planning trips to Mars to move away from the mess they made; politicians have their hands out waiting for the corporations to tell them what to say about the subject, and meanwhile, the poor and middle class are too poor or stuck in middle class to do anything about the future of life on this planet. We are in a great extinction period, and nothing is being done because even those citizens who know cannot do anything about it. They have to work so the corporations can make more money. But here we are, a group of kids, and we are doing something about the future of life on this planet. If we don't act now, it will be too late. It might already be too late, but we won't know until action is taken. We are the action."

The demands? The first one is that the President needs to declare a climate emergency and start action to fight global warming. All emissions need to start trending down now and eventually stop. Coal power plants need to be phased out within 2-4 years; fossil fuels need to be replaced within five years. The President must call for new action in the failing Paris Agreement. Pollution must be made illegal with a penalty minimum of twenty years. Publishing false information on global warming should be made illegal, and anyone who spreads propaganda about global warming should face up to 20 years in prison and pay back numerous fines.

And that is just the first page of demands. The total list of demands is 101, and each one as outlandish as the last. Yet despite these unachievable demands, Alice and her Moon Gang are doing what the scientists wouldn't, they are taking action.

The action has clearly gained attention from the White House as the President released a statement via social media calling for the "Owl Gang" to throw down their weapons, return power to the people of Kentucky, and come talk like adults. The president says this is the right approach and not "acting like we are a second world country."

The US government has a policy to not negotiate with terrorists, but these "terrorists" are underage, and have caused a power outage for nearly one million properties; they are holding two counties hostage, but claiming they are fighting for the future of life on this planet. It is an interesting conundrum considering all the scientists agree with the "Moonlighters in Kentucky."

Professor Steven Edwardson, a climate scientist working at Yale University, "We've been screaming for decades now, and nothing is being done. We've published papers, proved it is the biggest issue humans have ever faced, and yet nothing is being done. Now, maybe something will be done. Maybe."

As a heat wave moved in and covered the area of Louisville, Kentucky, the locals are suffering without air conditioning, three people have died, and they all toss around how much they hate the Moon Gang. Those that have a generator offer visits for those that don't, and the Kentucky Governor has shipped generators from other states to help maintain AC in public places like libraries, but the strain is hard on everyone. People are coming together to help one another, but there does not seem to be any sympathy for future generations.

Negotiations between the FBI and the Moon Gang have ceased. The four members inside the power plant are in a hurry up and wait period, and most locals believe the inevitable should happen now.

"Four kids with sawed off shotguns? We should just send in the local boys. That is what is going to happen anyway," Gary Charles, a Louisville born and bred man of 52 years. "We can't have a barbecue for the fourth, there is no air (conditioner), but it needs to end."

When I asked Mr. Charles if he felt any empathy for a group of teenagers trying to save the Earth from climate change he answered, "None at all. They don't even know if that is real, but I do know God made Adam and Eve not Adam and Steve." That sizzling sentiment seems to be resonating around the blazing hot city of Kentucky.

As the heat wave intensifies across the city, Louisvillians are eager to get the power restored, hoping a return to normalcy will happen before July 4th.

CHAPTER 32

Day 13, July Fourth

Dan Robinson called this morning to inform us that the rented residence where we held our Moonlighter meetings was destroyed. Goomba didn't understand at first, but he quickly realized Dan meant Mom's house. It was arson, and Mom's house was completely destroyed. The real kicker was Dan not mentioning if Mom was inside the house or not. He wouldn't confirm or deny it, and when I called him back, he said I could come out and find out for myself.

There was no way for me to get in touch with Mom so I held out hope that she was safe.

The patrons supporting our movement have grown tremendously. Fireworks were launched last night, and we've all been caught gawking at the pure number of supporters. Joey counted over a hundred, but it feels like a lot more.

Law enforcement isn't backing down from the crowd. Large trucks were brought in, and we are starting to see more troops which all assume is the national guard. It feels like only a matter of time until they bum rush the plant and the party ends.

Joey's paranoia seems to be coming to fruition; Dylan is spouting off similar phrases, and they two haven't been around each other in days.

"The end is near," Dylan said when I walked into his room this morning.

"That's a dire prediction I usually hear from the other portion of the castle." We'd been calling the power plant building the castle; it was fitting because troops were preparing to raid it.

"Yeah, well, look," Dylan handed me the binoculars.

"Look at what?"

"Those are army, or national guard, or super swat teams; I don't know which, but they are here now."

Glancing through the lenses, I saw soldiers, or men in fatigues moving in formation, or what appeared to be formation, but I couldn't see who or what they were.

"They could be here for the protestors. They've grown in numbers."

"Supporters you mean?"

"Yeah, do we know what's going on with them?"

"If you look that way," he pointed towards the far north area. "They have a home base area. I thought I saw X today, but it might have been someone else."

"There's a tent," I gasped. "I for sure saw X yesterday."

"Yeah, I think that tent is for the press though."

The number of supporters was already more than I could count and it wasn't even nine am.

"Did you hear about the house?" I asked him as I gave him back his binoculars.

"Yeah, Goomba said your mom wasn't inside; she wasn't right?"

"I don't know. Goomba was speculating based on the news not reporting anything."

"Did he hear anything on the police scanner about it?"

I shrugged.

"Is there any way to get a hold of your mom?"

"No, the phone here only goes out directly to Dan Robinson."

"You can call her on a burner."

"We've maintained radio silence this long; I think it is better to keep the status quo."

Dylan nodded, "Pam is safe, I know it."

"I hope so." I left.

Joey was even more tense. His shirt was off, and his BO was starting to be a problem too. The lack of showering was affecting all of us, but Joey was on another level. When I walked into the room, he was doing pushups.

"Happy July Fourth, or is it Happy Fourth of July?" He said still bouncing up and down with his pushup movements.

"I think it is - actually, I don't know."

"It doesn't matter," he jumped and looked out the window. "They are going to have to end this soon; the protestors are out in full force."

"Supporters."

"No, the supporters are people who support us; X was out there yesterday, and I think I caught Exel yesterday."

"Yeah, so who do you mean?"

"Now a gang is out protesting the supporters. Right wing nut jobs that even the local pigs called troublemakers."

"Where?"

There was a new group of people that were only visible through

Joey's window.

"They look like freaking cops to me," I said after studying them for a few minutes. "The cops really called them troublemakers?"

"Yeah, but you are probably right. They are probably off duty cops. It's an age-old tactic; they can get them to start something, and then they can use force against all the protestors."

"I have read something similar, but what can we do?"

"Nothing. Hopefully X and Exel and whoever else is out there sees it coming," Joey went back to doing pushups. "I heard about the house; Pam wasn't inside, right?"

I put the binoculars back down, "We don't know. I don't think so."

Joey stopped his pushups, laid on the ground, and flipped over so he was on his back and could begin doing sit ups. "That one asshole on the conservative station was calling for it."

"I know," I replied, but I was really worried about Mom.

"The public is restless; they will be coming in soon. Think about it, no power on the Fourth of July. The barbeques aren't the same. It's an American holiday."

"They can man the grills with charcoal," I added.

"They are coming in soon; I guarantee it!"

"Keep your eyes peeled," I said as I left. He was counting his sit ups.

Goomba's head was on his phone, but there was action on the camera screens behind him.

"Goomba, what's that?"

"Oh shoot," Goomba looked up and it was a group of folks nearing the entrance which was locked shut with two trucks parked in front of it. The police moved over and stopped the people as they shook the gate.

"They were trying to come inside," Dylan said through the walkie-talkie.

"Who is it?" I questioned, picking up Goomba's walkie talkie, I didn't wait for an answer. I ran towards Dylan.

Dylan responded as I ran, "I don't know, but the police stopped them. There was a lady leading them."

As I entered into Dylan's room, he informed me of signs he was reading, "One of them says, 'we are here to get our power back.'"

"Goomba, is there any other action on the cameras?" I asked the walkie-talkie.

"Nothing that I can see."

"They will be coming in soon," Dylan said.

Joey cut in from his talkie, "The police might not hold them back next time."

"Well, what do we do?" Dylan asked into his two-way, but he was looking at me.

"We haven't even got one demand met," Joey said through his talkie.

"Yeah, that needs to change. I am calling Dan."

The phone rang twice and Dan picked it up.

"Hello."

"Dan, what in the hell is going on down there?"

"Hello, well, I have to tell you this, we have a lot of locals here that want power. It is a national holiday, and these folks just endured one of the hottest heat streaks without AC. They are mad, and they tried to enter through the gates."

"Yeah, I saw them, so what's going on with our demands?"

"We are working on them," Dan Robinson responded, but I knew he was lying through his teeth.

"No you aren't. We got two hostages here, and if we don't hear anything soon, we take things into our own hands. We also have enough TNT to blow this place to hell and back so if those folks want power soon, you tell them we will blow it up so power isn't available ever again through this plant!"

I paused. I wanted to slam the phone down, but I also wanted to hear what Dan Robinson would say.

"Alice, don't go doing anything like that."

"The clock is ticking, Dan. You have our demands so make it happen, and keep those folks away from the gate."

He didn't hesitate to ask, "How much TNT do you have?"

I hung up.

"We aren't getting anything," I told Goomba before I spoke into his two-way, "Did they back up?"

"Yeah, they are backed up," Dylan responded.

"So what's the plan now?" Goomba asked; a sadness grew across his face.

"I don't know, Goomba, but you gotta keep your eyes on the cameras. Dylan can see the gate, but not like you can."

"Yeah, I know. I was watching that asshole," Goomba responded.

"Who?"

"The one who was calling for your mom's house to be burned down a few nights ago," Goomba showed me a video on his phone.

"Yeah, what's he saying now?"

"He's a night host, but he was called in to talk about your mom's house. He's an asshole so you know what he said."

"No, I don't know. The house is burnt down; what did he say?"

"Watch it," Goomba hit play on the video and handed me his phone.

There was the same conservative asshat with his hair slicked back.

"I've heard that the Moon house was burnt to the ground, and I know I did a hypothetical about that happening, but it was strictly that. I wasn't advocating for anyone to do that, and I can assure you that no one who watches my show would do that. It might have been someone connected to Nick Moon or perhaps his mother, Pam Moon, who burnt the house down themselves. It also might have been a fire from natural causes. Perhaps they are going to try to collect insurance money that way. I've heard of people doing that before, but if you go back and watch my hour long show, I only mentioned the house being burnt down briefly, and it wasn't advice. Although we are hearing that there is a lot of action outside the power plant in Kentucky today because folks are mad. They are mad because they don't have power, but it wasn't anyone who watches my show that did anything wrong. I barely mentioned it, and it is hard for me to remember if I did mention it or if it was a guest or what happened, but it did happen. All we know is the house might have burned down. We also know that millions do not have any electricity in the city and surrounding area of Lewisville, Kentucky, and the culprits, the crossdressing Nick Moon and his roadies are enjoying iced beverages. "

I shook my head, and slid the phone back to Goomba.

"It always goes back to the ice, why?"

"You're trying to find some sort of logic with these idiots? Don't bother."

CHAPTER 33

Two Weeks

Dan Robinson did not explicitly state that they would be coming in, but it was implied.

"They've amped up the guards, new trucks are here, and I can see them doing meetings," Joey informed me early this morning.

Last night we all went to the roof and watched as fireworks launched for miles and miles. It was the most light the area had seen since we took over. It was a beautiful view, and we joked about how not having any light for miles made the fireworks better. Joey even brought Curtis up, and we made a small fire so we could roast hot dogs we'd found in the breakroom fridge.

"You better double cook those dogs cause who knows how long they've been in there," Curtis warned us.

Curtis is a boomer who works at a coal plant and is as conservative as they come, but he is slowly warming up to our cause. It might be Stockholm Syndrome, but the man is definitely open to our ideas. He's also a guy who despises authority, as he's stated numerous times. He hasn't tried to escape once which is the part I find the strangest, but he's told Goomba numerous times that he doesn't want to die. We have all decided mutually that we won't kill him no matter what happens from here on out.

Cooking the hot dogs over a small fire with sticks felt about as normal as we'd felt since we arrived, and the pressure of everything seemed to lift for an hour or two.

"A bottle of Roby would be nice," Joey cackled as he said it, and we all joined him.

It was also the first time Joey and Dylan had been together since the beginning; they hadn't even shared a meal together because we always needed a watch somewhere, so they ate mostly by the window. Surprisingly, it went smoothly. The T-levels were down for an unknown reason, and there wasn't any animosity between them.

After we double-cooked the hot dogs, we ate them, watched the fireworks for a bit, but once the mosquitos began attacking, we all agreed it was time to head inside and head back to our posts. The fun was over.

I spent the evening watching a burner phone that Goomba filled with apps. Cable news was in a fury, and we were the main topic. We were minor celebrities, but it is more for being notorious than it is famous. We are hated by most, but starting to gain sympathy with a few pundits on the left-wing outlets. A lesbian with short black hair defended us:

"Over 300,000 thousand homes are still without power this Fourth of July in Louisville, Kentucky, and a heat wave reaching close to 100 degrees is calming as cooler winds and rain move into the area, but a bigger question is starting to emerge out of the area, and that is, why are these kids known as the Moonlighters or Moon Gang, doing this? The answer is simple, they are seeking answers themselves. This group of teenagers led by Alice Moon formerly Nick Moon, have listed their demands in a video online, and those demands are solutions to the climate crisis. All these teenagers want is action to be taken to protect life on this planet. That is all, and it seems scientists are agreeing with the Moonlighters. On tonight's show, we have a Harvard Professor and Climate Crisis specialist, who agrees that action needs to be taken, and he is agreeing with these Moonlighters."

The show isn't popular in Kentucky, and we didn't expect it to change any minds of those folks without power in Kentucky, but at least one side of the world was voicing our narrative.

The conservatives pundits were still bashing us, and also denying they called for Mom's house to be burnt down. It didn't matter though because the house was burned to ashes. The love from anyone felt good, as love does, but the message was clear from the conservatives.

A bowtied wearing conservative went in on us, but his guest for the night caused my jaw to drop.

"The radical libs are doing it again; they are trying to push this great country into a major depression with some sort of new green deal. The movement is starting in Kentucky of all places as Nick Moon, a crossing-dressing teenager,who was suspended from school for snoozing in class, is solely responsible for knocking out the power for close to a million homes. Nick Moon and his quote "Moon Gang" unquote, shot a security guard, and entered into the power plant armed to the T. They forced workers to shut down the power, which has now been off for two weeks. Electricity was cut off and a major heat wave took over the city. It has been terrible for the locals, and the demands of this Moon Gang are outlandish if not plain ignorant. They are asking for an end to coal power, an end to fossil fuels, a new Paris Agreement with other countries, and more.

These queer young men, who are all crossdressers, stormed into the power plant, and had the power cut while they themselves enjoyed power with help from a generator. They have a working ice maker while elderly folks have died because of the heat. Hypo-crits, all of them. These are merciless terrorists, hoodlums, and they need to be removed from the power plant yesterday. Remove them by force! Tonight, on our show, we are joined by a young man who partied with these terrorists a few times, and might have even been a member of the Moon Gang. His name is

Clark, and he is joining us from Lexington, Kentucky.

Good evening, Clark, how is everything?"

Clark looked different. His blue eyes still pierced through the screen, but he didn't look the same. He appeared scared as if he was forced to be on this show.

"Good evening."

"Clark, so tell us about Nick Moon, or as he calls himself, Alice Moon."

Clark: "Yeah, Nick was someone I met and I hung out with a few times. I wasn't aware of the plans to take out power for the whole city though."

"Right, so you hang out with Nick Moon, and tell us, did you attend any of these Thursday night bashes?"

Clark: "Yes, I did."

"Okay, and can you elaborate on what went on? We've heard it was full of gay orgies and crossdressing and drugs were used."

Clark: "No, it wasn't like that. The first time someone showed up, they had to drink a bottle of Robitussin to robo-trip, a cough syrup, but after that, it wasn't anything but sitting around the fire and talking about the collapse."

"Drinking the cough syrup? Does this have anything to do with what the rappers sing about? Sipping on some syrup?"

Clark: "I don't know, but I don't think so."

"You talked about the collapse so what is that?"

Clark: "The collapse of society, or I guess the impending doom that is coming in from climate change."

"From the climate? These goons are the only ones causing the collapse. They knocked the damn power out and sent their local society back to the stone ages. The hypocrisy… Do you understand that the weather always changes?"

Clark: "Yes, I do, but the main discussion at these parties was the man-made climate crisis."

"There isn't a lot of proof that it is man-made, Clark. You do understand this, right?"

Clark: "Yes, I do now."

"So it was discussion propaganda, sipping on cough medication, which is likely terrible for the kidney and livers, and crossdressing."

Clark: "Something like that."

"Okay, so you said the first time someone attended they had to drink a whole bottle of Robitussin?"

Clark: "They didn't have too, because I know a few that didn't, but it was kind of a requirement."

"Really, so Clark did you do this?"

Clark: "Yes."

"Okay, and Clark tell us about crossdressing. This Nick Moon was really into dressing like a woman, right? He was even seen at school dressed up as a woman, and he calls himself Alice when he does it."

Clark: "Yes, it was something he did, and a few others did, but not everyone. I never did, and it should be noted that it wasn't a homosexual party. Not everyone at these parties was homosexual."

"Okay Clark, so tell us, this Moon Gang, what are they trying to accomplish?"

Clark: "They really think climate change is real and that it is man-made, and they think they can stop it. They are on a mission to raise awareness about it. That is what they want to do.”

“So by cutting power to millions, they want to raise awareness?”

Clark: “Yes, Alice believes if they do something to show others that things can be done, even if they are extreme, that they can or will get followers who will try to do things too.”

“So they are looking for copycat criminals to also shut down the power to cities?”

Clark: “I don’t know if Alice wants that exactly but something similar.”

“And when you say Alice, you are referring to Nick?”

Clark: “Yes, Nick is Alice.”

“So this Moon Gang has killed one security guard, and another quote hostage unquote is also dead, power is out for millions, and has been for two weeks now, and let me ask you Clark, we are hearing the populus is very annoyed, are the people going to rise up and storm the power plant?”

Clark: “I don’t know. People are pretty upset.”

“You bet they are! The FBI is going to be on these boys like a tick on a deer! Thanks for joining us tonight, Clark. The Moon Gang is a scary group of young, crossdressing terrorists who I would compare to the Taliban, but I am glad that you didn’t get involved with them anymore than a few forced drinks of Robitussin cough syrup.”

Clark: “Thanks.”

CHAPTER 34

Day 15

I was running in a field of gold wheat with the sun shining high and rainbows on either side of me. The sky was blue, and Alice was running with me. Across her face a large smile, and a row of ducks in a perfect V above us was leading the way.

I should have known I was dreaming in such a perfect world.

"I got movement; straight ahead and off the left," Dylan said, but it didn't wake me up or register in my sleeping brain. I only turned and looked at the rainbow, and behind it was a quarter moon.

The shots of tear gas and shattering glass didn't move me either.

Mom's voice crept into my dream, "The moon is back at a quarter to remind you to cut your toenails."

She said it every month when the crescent moon crept into our vision. The sun disappeared, and darkness rolled over us.

Joey's voice barked through the CB into my dream, "They are coming in!"

"What's the plan now?" Goomba begged, but I wasn't waking up. "What do we do now?"

The window in my office room shattered, and a can crashed on the floor and rolled across the tile until it smashed into my feet on the carpeted area. Smoke fell from the can and it quickly rose. It happened so quickly that I had no idea what was going on. It did wake me up, though.

Tear gas burns the inner part of the nose behind the eyes; it also burns the eyes, but when tear gas hits the nose, it feels like hot coals. Tears flow but it doesn't help the matter. My vision was destroyed, and it somehow turned my other senses off too. I could taste the basic chemical, but it hurt the worst when it entered my lungs. The agonizing pain that was inside my nose became like a mild paper cut to a sword incision of my chest. I huffed hard for air only to bring in more tear gas.

"Holy fuck," I tried to say into the two-way, but it came out more as, "hole-E-uck."

Coughing didn't help so I covered my face with my shirt. Dashing away from the two canisters with smoke exiting them, I ran smack into Goomba who was running towards me. He was wearing his shirt around his face, and we both fell to the ground in opposite directions.

"Jeez, Alice, now what?"

"Come in here, I will tie you up!"

I helped Goomba up, and I shoved him back into the room I'd just exited. Somehow, I found the duct tape roll; I yanked out a long portion of it, and began to tie his hands together. The roll tape was still attached to the roll, but I stretched it around his hands and feet.

"Freeze, get your hands up!"

I heard the blasting of gunshots, but the voices were coming from the two-way.

I shoved Goomba to the floor, "sit down!"

Running back into the hallway, I saw Dylan running towards me. He was holding the sawed off shotgun. It was over.

"Drop your weapons; surrender, surrender!" I screamed into the two-way.

Dylan disappeared; smoke surrounded me. I walked slowly into the main room with the cameras, they were black; there is no doubt the Feds cut them first.

Standing in the main office, the noises stopped, and the smoke rose quietly. I listened and waited, hearing only my heartbeat in my chest thumping with fear. Then I heard the ticking of the clock on the wall. The battery operated old school round clock was running as if not a care in the world; both hands were stopped for a slight second as I read it, it was perfectly five am.

"Freeze! Get your hands up!"

I put my hands to the sky and waited to be tackled.

The Feds raided the plant at 4:57 am, and by 5:01 we were all in handcuffs and Curtis rescued. The tear gas remained in my nose and lungs for days. Only Joey fired his weapon, but it was a random shot that wasn't even aimed. We were all taken without injury to anyone. Goomba was handcuffed briefly, but by the time I saw him outside, as I was being hauled away in the back of a State Troopers car, a female paramedic was putting something in his eyes to help with the burning.

"It worked," I said to myself.

When I was tackled, it was excessively aggressive for a man with his hands up. My shoulder slammed into the ground, and as I lay on the ground, the butt of a rifle found my face. A boot found my back and held me down while the man leaned into my face and spit into my ear, "Faggot, we got ya now."

My dress was ripped when I was forced to stand up, and I was thrown against the wall while my hands were held behind my back. The SWAT team was dressed in all black with black guns and black masks to protect from the tear gas.

Joey, Dylan, and I were all separated, but the only words I

muttered were, "I want to speak with my attorney."

I was searched, handcuffed, and forced to exit the building with my dress ripped down the left side and barefoot. The handcuffs were so tight on my wrists that my fingers turned white. Two cops ushered me outside, and I was forced to walk briskly over the gravel towards a car. There was no sign of Joey or Dylan at this point, and I feared they might be dead.

My head hit the top of the car as I was put into the backseat of the trooper's car.

When I saw Goomba, he was cuffed, but they quickly took them off and he was offered medical treatment. Joey was bleeding, his shirt was off, and he was being pushed by two guards as he cussed them out. It was a much cooler arrest; he was more defiant than I was, but he was in the same situation. He was placed into a squad car across from me.

Dylan came out next, and he wasn't as uncooperative. He walked slowly, but the coppers tossed him anyway. Three guards picked him up, and carried him head first into the edge of a cop car. His head slammed into it before a door was opened, and he was tossed like bad meat into the backseat.

Curtis exited the building last wrapped in a blanket, and his eyes were dropping puddles of water. The medical staff ran over to him, and they began to pour milk into his eyes. He slumped to the ground, and continued to cry. He was free, and I felt good about that considering.

It was over. Our mission had failed to gain even one of our demands. We'd been swept out of the power plant in ten minutes and were on our way to jail in twenty. We'd be facing life or worse, and we'd accomplished nothing.

A pointy head State Trooper jumped into the driver's seat and without saying a word hit the gas.

I was defeated, and it only grew as the car exited the plant, and fists slammed the back window.

I fell back in fear.

"They caught him!"

The protesters to our mission were in full force, and beating on the windows as we pulled away. Their slurs were muffled, but I felt their hatred through the glass. They wanted to rip my bones apart one by one.

"Let us have the faggot!"

Our motive wasn't to enrage people, it was to inspire them. As the car drove through the crowd of protesters, rocks pounded the windows, and middle fingers flew at me, I knew the whole operation was a failure.

It was already a failure when Jackson and the guard died, but now their deaths wouldn't even be worth anything.

Rocks and fists pounded on the two other cars as Dylan and Joey were rushed through. I turned to watch it, and a woman from the press snapped a photo of me looking back.

We failed. Jackson died for nothing and the security guard too.

I hung my head as the car took me to jail. I was booked, and told I would never see free daylight again. And for what? Nothing. I failed. And not just Jackson dying, but Dylan and Joey would also be tossed into a cage for the rest of their lives.

Failure at that extreme can only be met with suicide.

CHAPTER 35

Last night a rope was left in my cage. I call it a cage because the solitary room I am locked inside is big enough to house a small dog. It wasn't just a rope, it was also a black belt. Belts are removed from all prisoners when they are booked into the jail, and rope is taken away long before booking and usually before the arrest. The reason belts are removed and ropes are banned is because it becomes a liability for the jail if someone hurts themselves.

That liability disappeared last night. The jail or someone who works here wouldn't mind if I hurt myself. It appears they wanted it. I returned from the showers, and the two items were on my cot.

When the door shut and locked behind me, I didn't even look at either one. I saw them, but I am still getting adjusted to my surroundings, and even in a tiny cell like this, I didn't put one and two together. Not that it mattered anyway; I didn't have a phone to call room service or anything.

It didn't take long for me to figure out why these two objects were placed in my cage. Someone, if not everyone, wanted me to use the rope and belt. And I won't lie and say it didn't cross my mind. Every thought I'd had since arriving inside my cage was focused on the failure of a mission that I led.

Jackson was dead. He'd never become a mechanic. He'd never taste a frozen snicker again, his favorite, and he'd never get to do anything. The weight of that wore on me. It tore at me like two horses pulling me apart. I also thought about Dylan and Joey, and how they were as good as dead too. I did more than think about it, I played with the rope and the belt. I tugged the rope, and framed the belt into the shape of my neck.

Why would they want me to kill myself? It would be a huge liability, and so on, I wondered, but it finally hit me.

They didn't mind if I became a martyr. If I died right now, there would be no trial, no press, and they could brandish me as a crossdressing, bisexual who was crazed and needed god. But if I lived, and had a trial, it was another chance to raise awareness. I could tell my side of the story! But only if I survived this rotten jail that is.

I still feared guards might enter my cell, wrap the belt around my neck, tie it to the rope, and hang me. The fear lasted all night, and when the guards opened the doors in the morning, I'd been up all night trying to think of a way to let everyone know I didn't die from suicide.

Luckily, I wasn't killed. The guards fed me breakfast, and then they took me down to meet with my public 'pretender' Mr. B.G. James Worthy. It was all I could afford, meaning I couldn't afford anyone, but at least I'd survived the night and would get a trial.

When I told Mr. Worthy about the presents delivered to my cage, he nodded, stared away and muttered, "Ah, a tactic dating back thousands of years," as if we should both just accept it.

My stomach did a somersault.

"You'll be fine as long as you don't use it."

That was only the second most insane thing he said all morning. The first was, "we don't want to utilize your trial as a way to get a message out."

He wasn't going to let me testify at my trial, and I had no clue I could change attorneys. I didn't have a dime nor an inkling of knowledge about how the justice system worked. I did understand the phrase, "I was fucked," because, well, I was.

When I returned to my cell, the rope and belt were gone. The county had tried the trick and I'd survived. I'd get my trial, but according to my attorney, I wouldn't get to make even a whimper. However, it was still preferable to death.

I didn't know everything hit the fan that afternoon, and it wouldn't start to really hit the fan for one more day. The process started, and I was alive. I'd hear about it soon, but I slept without the fear of a belt and rope in my cage.

CHAPTER 36

The news reported it incorrectly, but when it was corrected, they wished they had kept the incorrect report. A few news outlets never corrected it. Operation FDIC or Phase II of our plan started with only that hitch; the local news reporting a fire at a bank. It wasn't a fire, it was a grenade that caused fire.

Cherry kept her word and continued our mission. She did this despite local sentiment against us, and despite it appearing like our movement was dead. Cherry was the only Moonlighter to not be interviewed, and one has to think that played a role too. It's unclear how the FBI missed her.

A flawless plan can only succeed with a perfect execution. X and Rex operated with perfection, and they were able to do so without communicating with each other because of a fear that the feds were watching. The other Moonlighters involved carried out their roles marvelously too.

Just before noon, Cherry arrived at the bank building just off of Bardstown Road, and she began filming different scenes revolving around a bank canister device and a hand grenade. She pulled the pin to the grenade, placed it into the canister, and pressed the button to send it flying through the vacuum tube into the bank. The grenade detonated. Cherry was filming, and Phase II aka Operation FDIC was underway.

Cherry's video didn't look like she placed the canister into the tube, but it looked like someone else did and she was filming it. Her footage was superb, and she did so without the help of anyone else. She filmed the explosion, and then uploaded it to a social media account shared on four platforms with the username, HansonFan1 and CherryVsCapitolists. These four accounts had almost one million followers and subscribers.

After the footage was online, she went live on social media, and she remained calm and stoic like a trained actress as she proclaimed, "Oh my god, this man came inside the bank, tried to withdraw his money, but he was denied. The teller was like, we don't have that much, so he came outside, grabbed what appeared to be a grenade, and put it into the drive-thru thingy, and sent it into the bank. It blew up. I guess he was making a deposit and not a withdrawal. Jesus. Go look at my other videos, and look!"

Pointing the camera from her car into the bank showed a fire behind the bulletproof glass. This video was seen by nearly 200,000 people in fifteen minutes.

Before X entered into a bank with another name in Oak Park, Illinois just shy of Chicago, he opened his phone and went live to an audience built up of 330,000 subscribers. X's username was "BellaOneTwo3" and the profile pics were all of Bella. Almost 10,000 watched his livestream as he entered the bank and began yelling.

"I can't take out my money? It is my money!"

His phone camera panned to show the tellers behind the desk, and one yelled out, "Sir!"

He turned his phone so it faced up at the ceiling and he began to speak while walking, "They said they cannot let me pull out my money! It is my money. My fucking money! The bank says they don't have the money, and I can take out ten grand, but not the one hundred grand that is mine!"

He turned the camera to a small piece of wood that read, "Your Money is Insured by the FDIC up to 200,000."

X smacked the small, wooden piece across the room, "Yeah, but I cannot take it out!"

The recording ended, and X wisely linked Cherry's video as he exited the bank.

Rex was in the panhandle of Florida, and he armed his live feed as he exited a bank in the panhandle. His account name across all his social media accounts was RoboTrippy and had over 700,000 subscribers total.

Rex wore a fake mustache and glasses, and he spoke without his twang, "The bank just told me I cannot withdraw my money because they don't have it! Can you believe this bullshit! They don't have my freaking money!"

His camera zoomed to show the front of the bank, and then he showed a withdrawal slip in his hand with the amount $125,000.00 on it.

"Let me show you my account with this bank!"

The camera panned to show the name of the bank, and then he crumpled a piece of paper out of his pocket; it showed the same bank name on the top of the paper, and he quickly scanned to the bottom of the paper. It was his bank statement, and it showed he had $276,989.06 in it.

Rex's stream was watched by 130,000 people live.

The world began to tune in, as the videos were shared, watched, and commented at a record pace, and within five minutes of each being posted, they had combined over one million views. By the time 12:30 rolled around the three videos were over ten million streams and the number was doubling every seven minutes.

It didn't matter that the third comment on Cherry's video read, "That bank isn't even open right now." The bank wasn't open, but it appeared open. Cherry's uncle owned the building, and it was being restored to open as a bank in a month. The person in charge of cleaning it out was Cherry.

The videos soared across all social media with the false message that the banks were out of money. A lie on social media became a truth once it hit a million views. The Moonlighters were behind the scenes pulling off the biggest hoax in the history of ever, and there was no way to stop it. By the time anyone realized it was all fake, a run on the banks was happening, and once a run on the banks is really happening, it only triggers more folks to run on the banks.

Across America banks were ambushed by anxious customers who wanted to withdraw everything. Bank tellers clocked out, bank security men locked the doors, but that didn't help the narrative. People flooded into the banks, ATMs were emptied at a record pace, and the false news that the banks didn't have the money became a truth. The banks didn't have the money because everyone was coming at once. Crowds mobbed through the streets, and in New York City, one mob headed towards Wall Street. Chaos was upon the great United States.

The banks and wall street execs who'd made millions lying about the threat of global warming, or perhaps lying about some other thing to get rich, began to sweat at the fear of losing everything. The President shut down the Nasdaq and Dow Jones as it approached a record drop in just two hours. Those who got their money out safely ran for cover, but most Americans ran for their guns; a predicted response.

Before the banks closed, the frenzied mobs ran for the groceries.No one knew what was next; it was pure pandemonium in the streets. Grocery stores across the country were flooded with so many people that they too had to close, but they couldn't. As long as food was visible and a brick nearby, the groceries were open.

Glass was shattered and doors pried opened. A mob mentality flew through the country, and storms of people took out whole grocery stores in seconds. These tame folks who left work wondering what was going on were now savages, unleashed into a new world, and they didn't want to miss out on anything, especially not their next meal.

Those that weren't looting, were rioting for fun, and those that were still at home turned into social media where everything was being recorded. It was a fire sale, and everything was being sold.

A man with his tie tied around his head like a headband, led a mob through the Oxmoor Mall. He had the look of a man sitting at a cubicle only hours before, but now he was leading a tribe through the mall on a witch hunt for a stockbroker to blame and hang! The people behind him were chanting, and tearing down any camera while starting fires. Oxmoor Mall wasn't going to survive the hour.

Two camera's filmed this man as he led the people through the mall. The first was username, CubicleFighter, which was surely the man's own account despite it having 450,000 followers, and the other was username Exel_BearCat. The man leading the charge was none other than Exel. He'd never worked in a cubicle or worn a tie in his entire life besides his grandmother's funeral.

His video streamed live to over two million people.

The Oxmoor Mall burned to the ground, and the police watched as the mob behind Cubicle Man grew, and they headed towards St. Matthews Mall to show that one mall wasn't better than the other.

The department stores were looted, raided by pirates who were thirsty to burn name brands. A rallying cry rose from the crowd to do just this. The people were angry, and Exel directed their anger right into these corporations who designed purses and pants and then charged a mark up of $800 dollars while having slave labor in India or China or Vietnam create it.

#FucktheBrands began trending on several social media platforms as the most expensive items inside the mall were tossed into the fire pits outside.

A second live stream showed a young lady wearing a pantsuit leading a new army of former mall goers through a mall in Indianapolis. The Fashion Mall at Keystone suffered the same fate as the Oxmoor Mall. The username was OwlRebellion.

The Moonlighters were doing it, and I was sitting inside a cage without a clue. But I do have to admit even if you would have told me it was happening, I wouldn't have believed it. I thought our movement was dead in the water, but it wasn't. It was alive, and it was happening across the country.

The viral hashtags of #WhereisMyMoney, #FuckBrands, and #FuckWallStreet slowly turned into the #OwlRebellion and it became the most trending word in the history of all trending words. The Owl Rebellion was born, and it flooded across all social media platforms like a tsunami.

Before seven pm, the President declared a state of emergency and a national curfew. The national guard was called, but nobody answered. Most of the men and women who served the guard were out fighting the system, and those that weren't were watching live on TV as 209 malls across the country burned to the ground; 1800 grocery stores were looted; 306 banks were looted or burned, hundreds of gas stations were lit on fire, restaurants with a corporation name were destroyed, and 12 police headquarters were burned to the ground.

Chaos covered the streets. It was a real life purge.

And before the clock rolled into midnight, a new viral hashtag began to appear online, and it stayed for most of the night as things slowly quieted across the country.

That hashtag #FreeAlice

CHAPTER 37

By the time order was restored, folks went home wondering what they just did, and those at home watching wondered what they'd just seen. Some described it as a civil war, others described it as the collapse, but a Time Magazine staff writer described it the best when she wrote, "it felt like the end of the world's riots."

The approval rating of the Moonlighters and our mission was sky high as the banks collapsed, but once order was restored, the lines went back to being divided against us. We did have a larger following on our side. We weren't the huge enemy of all people anymore. That's not to say we were loved by all because we weren't. Even some of those who rioted against the system weren't on board just 12 hours later. Some of those folks were just a part of the mob, some just loved the anarchy, and some feared the end was near and acted accordingly.

It was the old adage of, if everyone jumped off a bridge, would you? It had a few new stipulations, and the question was now, if everyone raged against the capitalist evil-overlords that control everything would you? And it turns out that a lot of folks did. Yet when order was restored, and folks could tune back into their propaganda screens, most went back to normal. The troubles and pains of trying to start a 21st century rebellion!

Meanwhile, back in my 2x2 foot cage, I didn't have any knowledge of what was happening. Most of the rioting took place in large cities, and I was stuck forty-five minutes from my hometown of Louisville. Also, I was inside the 2x2 cage. (Okay, so it wasn't two by two, but it sure felt like it.)

None of this mattered to the authorities because they were blaming me for the riots. The media, pundits, and those who sympathized with these big corporations begin the slander. My face was plastered everywhere, and I became the whipping boy. I didn't mind, though, because I didn't know; the hashtag-Free-Alice movement needed to be squashed.

Well, I didn't know until I met with my attorney.

Mr. Worthy was sweating when he walked into our meeting room, and he said, "if you weren't in deep shit before, you are now."

"I think I was before," I reminded him.

"Yeah, but after everything that happened in the last 24 hours, I would say they are about to throw the book at you. The death penalty might be easier for you now, son."

"What? Why? What happened?"

"The goddamn Owl Rebellion your Moon Gang started last night!"

"What?"

"I guess you have been in a cave all night; here take some coffee."

He was so shaken up by the events the night before, he brought me coffee but forgot to offer it to me.

"What happened?" I begged, but I also reached for the coffee. I needed it.

"Massive riots, looting, whole cities burned to the ground!" His eyebrows exploded with each word, and he shook his head back and forth. "It was like a war, a civil war, but there was nothing civil about it."

"Really?" I sipped the cold brew and tried to not act surprised.

I was surprised even though we'd planned it, I didn't think it would happen.

"Yes, really! The whole country is in a state of emergency. There is a nationwide curfew, I passed freaking tanks on the way here! Freaking tanks!"

"Freaking tanks, huh? Why?"

"Why? You know why! Because of your damn Owl Rebellion. There was a run on the banks yesterday afternoon and that escalated things, and well the escalating of things got pretty bad. Louisville is on fire right now! The malls in the east end are nothing more than ashes."

"I didn't have anything to do with that; I was sleeping in my cage all night."

"Yeah, well, they are saying it was the Moon Gang who started it."

"The Moon Gang? So Joey and Dylan aren't in jail?"

"No, well, yes, of course they are in jail, but the other members of the Moon Gang."

"There aren't any other members!"

"That's not the word on the streets. The FBI is going to be making arrests. People are dead. It was a battlefield last night! It was like a world war, I am telling you."

"A world war would imply it is happening across the world, by different countries."

"You know what I mean! The whole country was a madhouse, and we are under orders from the President himself to get you in front of the camera to call for peace."

"Me? To call for peace? Peace for what? Is there a war? Do I have troops on my side? I am stuck in a two by two cage all day and night except when I come in here!"

"Yeah, well it doesn't freaking matter. The Vice President contacted us this morning, and a reporter is coming over to interview you. They want you to tell them to squash the rebellion."

"Squash what rebellion? Who should I tell?"

"The goddamn Owl Rebellion! Did you not hear me? I said the freaking Vice President contacted me!"

The coffee was cold so I was sipping away at it like it would leave if I didn't; I took one long sip before saying, "Yeah, but first you said the President and now you are saying the Vice President."

"So? The President ordered the Vice to do it; it doesn't matter. They have talking points, and they want to get you on the air denouncing everything. Tell people the owl rebellion is supposed to be peaceful, tell folks to stand down. We need peace and order in this country."

"I am not running a rebellion; I can assure you of that. I'm in a cage 23 hours a day. And I cannot tell people to stand down, I don't have any people. My two best friends, Joey and Dylan, are locked up in cages too."

"It doesn't matter what you admit; you need to tell folks to stand down!"

"What kinda shit is this? This doesn't sound very much like America, you know the country that doesn't negotiate with terrorists. Last week the President wouldn't give me the time of day, but now he wants me to do this?"

"It's probably the VP's idea, but it doesn't matter. It is an order! And as long as the order is restored, they won't even run the interview. They just want it in case things pop off again like they did yesterday."

"Yeah? How are the banks doing?"

"Banks are closed! Wall Street is freaking closed. It is worse than it was on 9-11! There was no order yesterday; groceries were raided, police stations destroyed! I don't think you understand the type of shit that you started. We need it to end, and it needs to end now."

I grimaced my lips into a curl, "I thought you said it was over?"

"Son, yes, it doesn't matter, but we are under orders, and you will agree with the orders and denounce the Owl Gang."

"I thought you said it was the Owl Rebellion?"

"Whatever!"

"You said, the Owl Gang," I was messing with him. "Do I denounce the owl gang or the owl rebellion?"

"Mr. Moon, this is very serious; I need you to sign this, and we are preparing your interview now."

"My interview? It will be televised?"

"Yes, the cameras will come into this room, and so will a reporter to ask you staged questions."

"Staged questions?"

"Yes, we have them, and you will need to - "

I cut him off, "Do I have to stay in this shitty outfit? Can you get me a dress like the one I had?"

"No! No! No! Mr. Moon, you need to take this seriously, if you don't comply, your trial, your sentencing, it will all change. It all hinges on this very moment. You're being labeled a terrorist"

"I already was."

He read me some of the staged questions, but I didn't

acknowledge him at all; I only smiled. My plan worked, and my entire body filled with an ecstasy. We had done it.

I didn't care what happened next.

CHAPTER 38

The interview never ran on the air. Anyone with half a brain knew it wouldn't see the light of day legally, but somehow, it was leaked online. The US Government wasn't going to let me speak to the people, but it didn't help that I wouldn't stick to the script. The young lady they sent to interview me, Ms. Connie Hawkins, had no previous interview experience. She had zero interviews anywhere online, and my hyperbolic speculation was that she was planted by the government.

Ms. Hawkins' demeanor was nonthreatening, almost like she wanted to come off as a preschool teacher; she spoke with a soft voice. The interview took place in the same room where I met with my attorney, and it happened quickly; it wasn't even nine am when she strolled in with a camera man.

"Should I call you Nick or Alice?"

"Either one is fine." I wasn't happy about anything, but this was putting me in a bad mood.

Her cameraman was tall and slim, and knew his voice was best not captured; he set up quickly and she jumped right into it.

"So you were born Nickalous Warren Moon, but you often go by Alice. Can you tell us about that?"

"Is it important?"

"I think some people want to know the answer. Are you a crossdresser? Do you want to transition?"

"I am just a person. I am human."

"But you do like to wear women's clothes?"

"Yes, I think I look fantastic in a dress."

"So you're a crossdresser?"

"Do we need labels like that right now?"

"Are you a gay male who likes to wear a dress?"

"I am just a human."

"But you are gay, can you say you are homosexual?"

"What's the definition?"

"A homosexual is a person attracted to their own sex, so in your case a male attracted to males."

"Sure, that fits sometimes, but not all the time."

"So you are bisexual?"

"Bi means two, right? Like a bicycle is two-tired. I guess I am two, sometimes I am Nick, sometimes I am Alice."

"No, that would be closer to bipolar; are you bipolar?"

"What's the definition of bipolar?"

"I am sorry; I don't have that exactly with me right now. Have you ever been diagnosed with bipolar?"

"No, but why does it matter?"

"It matters because people are interested in you, and because they want to know."

"This really shouldn't be about me or who I have sex with. It shouldn't matter. What I wear should not matter either. This isn't about me. This is about the future of our planet, and how action needs to start now."

"So is that why you wear the dress?"

"I wore the dress because I wanted to wear it. It wasn't a fashion statement, but if it did bring in more attention to our cause then that is a good thing."

"So do you want to transition into a female?"

"I don't see how that matters."

"Again, it matters because people want to know about you."

"It doesn't matter. If I do, I do. This isn't about the pronoun war that the right wing media wants it to be; this is about the end of life on this planet. The corporations in this country are enabling it if not outright causing it, and I am sick of the narrative that global warming or climate change is fake. It isn't fake, it is fossil fuels causing it, all the scientists know this, and yet none of them are acting on it."

"So you felt like you should act on it?"

"Yes, and now people are waking up to it."

"Waking up? So are you waking them up?"

"Yes! I hope so, anyway. People need to wake up, and realize that life is in trouble."

"So you're part of the woke mob?"

"The woke mob? I don't even know what that is."

"You are waking people up, so?"

"No, look, people need to know, I can change the semantics here. People need to be aware of everything that happens, and right now, fossil fuels are destroying this planet."

"So with everything that has happened in the last 24 hours, -"

"I don't know what has happened because I have been inside a cage in Bullitt County Jail.”

“Surely you’ve been told about what has happened?”

“I was told minutes ago; I’ve been locked in a cage all night.”

“The Owl Rebellion is what some people are calling what happened last night.”

“I was told.”

“Your name is associated with the movement, so even if you do not have anything to do with it, do you denounce the movement?”

“How can I denounce something I don’t have anything to do with?”

“It seems like it would be really simple to do.”

“And what is this Owl Rebellion?”

“Mr. Moon, you took power from millions of people, and you placed a white sheet with an owl on it outside the power plant that you took over to do this.”

“So that means I started this Owl Rebellion?”

“A hashtag trending last night was Free Alice.”

“I am not free.”

“Tanks are outside the jail so any attempts to free you were likely stopped.”

“It’s hard for me to lead a rebellion from a prison cell isn’t it?”

“Yes, but it should be easy for you to denounce it.”

I shook my head, “what is the reason for the Owl Rebellion?”

“It is unknown, but some are tying it to your cause of shutting down the power.”

"So it is tied to my cause, and we shut down the power to raise awareness about the climate crisis. We demanded action, but it didn't happen."

"So if it is tied to your movement do you denounce it?"

"If the actions taken across the country yesterday are tied to what we did, you want me to denounce it?"

"Yes."

"If people are finally acting up because they want to end the climate crisis, I will not denounce it. I will cheer them on."

"We won't air this video if you do not."

"Then do not air it. You came here to me, and you wanted me to call down folks who are finally acting on climate change? No way! You came here and you asked if I am a crossdressing homosexual, which is irrelavent to anything, and now you want to -"

"Cut the camera; we are done here."

"Oh, we are done here? So are you finished or are you done?"

"We are both finished and done!" Ms. Hawkins stood up, and removed her microphone from the front of her blouse.

"Good, but let me assure you and the President, that I will not stop until action is taken."

"You've been stopped."

"Yes, I have, but the people who began yesterday haven't."

I didn't budge from my seat.

"So you do admit the action yesterday was taken on your behalf?"

"No."

"Or you don't want to be held liable?"

"If the Owl Rebellion is happening, I love it. I want it to succeed! I will not call for it's -"

The camera faded to black, and the interview never ran on the air. It did leak to social media a few weeks later during my trial. The general assumption is that it was leaked by someone who was a sympathizer with the Owl Rebellion. It didn't cause that much of a ruckus though. My trial wasn't televised, and things looked really grim by the time it leaked.

CHAPTER 39

My case against the Commonwealth of Kentucky was what prosecutors call an "open and shut case." I was found guilty by a jury of my peers, and thanks to my attorney, Mr. Worthy, I didn't even get a chance to speak until after I was found guilty on all counts. The jury only debated for one hour and twenty two minutes; a record for a case this big, or at least one pundit said so.

Mr. Worthy whispered into my ear right before the jury returned, "if they look you in the eyes, it usually means they liked you and you will be found innocent."

"Usually? Have you ever had it not be the case?" I whispered back.

"Yeah, if they really want you to fry."

When the jury took their seats, all eyes were on me; I felt as though I ought to address them in some way. It turns out, I wasn't in the "usual" list of Mr. Worthy's clients, and the jury wanted me to fry.

The jury of my peers was eight men and four women. Together the twelve had two high school diplomas and four GEDs. The twelve jurors didn't even know global warming was a thing, and if they did they assumed it was left-wing propaganda to push through a new green deal.

The prosecuting team used trigger words at the undereducated jurors when talking about me: bipolar, transgendered, crossdressing, homosexual, gay, crazed, insane, queer, liberal, radical, and more. They labeled me crazy, but I couldn't pull the insanity card.

All twelve were staring at me when they entered the courtroom.

Guilty. Guilty, Guilty.

When I turned around to give Mom a signal, two coppers pulled me upright and I couldn't even get back around to see her again. She was crying even though she faked a smile when our eyes did finally meet. I nodded at her as the courtroom coppers pulled me away.

Neither Dylan or Joey turned over on me even though I wrote letters to both of them. "Get yourself a lighter sentence, please! Testify against me," I begged in my letters. They didn't. As a courtesy of the commonwealth, we were all tried separately. The prosecutors who read my letters wanted my trial to happen first so they'd have some time to get one of them to turn. But they never did.

They rushed me away quickly from the courthouse back to the jail, and as I walked through the underground area back to the jail, the press was waiting for me. One of them yelled out, "was it worth it, Nick?"

"Hell yeah!"

My reply wasn't clever enough to make the headlines, but a few articles quoted me as saying I would do it again which is typical. I would do it again, but I'd do a lot of things differently.

27 days later, it was finally my time to speak, and I came prepared. Worthy told me to beg for forgiveness, admit my ideology was screwed up, and inform the judge I'd learned my lesson. And I finally told Worthy where to go with it.

"Your honor, thank you for letting me speak before you sentence me. I was informed by my legal counsel to tell you that I learned my lesson, and that my ideology was screwed up, and that of course, I am sorry for my actions. I will not say those things."

A hush fell over the courtroom, but I didn't stop for more than a second.

"I am only sorry that Jackson was killed, and I do feel some guilt that the guard, Tommy, died too. Tommy killed Jackson first, and I acted in a mad state of revenge after that. That should be noted because that is how it happened. I also feel some guilt for the elderly folks who died during the heatwave, but I can assure you worse is coming. We didn't want anyone to die, and as you know, I even committed another crime, stealing solar panels to try to help the hospitals keep up. Anyone with that type of foresight should be given some leeway on an accidental death later. We didn't want anyone to die.

I wanted to create awareness for something the scientists agree 99% on, and something that is already happening. Humans are destroying life on this planet. Period. That statement is all factual. The only way to end the incoming collapse of the civilized world is to have action yesterday, and that action will never come. That, your honor, is what this was all about; we wanted to raise the stakes, and push people to fight back. Every single scientist agrees this is coming, and I know I said 99% early, so there is 1% that doesn't, but show me anything else with that high of number in agreement."

I paused to flip through my notes, which was difficult in handcuffs, and the judge ripped into me.

"I've heard enough; you aren't sorry; you aren't going to belittle the courtroom with this 99% of the scientists agree? They agree what? That the planet is warming up?"

"Yes, your honor, 99% of all scientists believe global warming aka climate change aka the climate crisis is man-made and it is going to destroy life on this planet!"

"99%? Well, Mr. Moon, I am not a scientist, and this is my

courtroom. If the good lord wants the world to get hotter, it will get hotter, and if he doesn't, it won't. I am a Christian, and that's the only fact that matters! God willing."

A few folks clapped after he said his Christian line. The judge asked for order, slammed his gavel down, and then he sentenced me. That's when I lost it, and the soundbyte was created.

"The end is coming, and we caused it!"

"Order!" The judge barked as he banged his gavel down.

"And we fucking deserve it," I snapped.

"The end is coming, it is man made, and if we don't act we deserve it!"

CHAPTER 40

Transportation from Bullitt County Jail to the prison in Eddyville, Kentucky is a pretty standard procedure. The van makes trips three times a month, usually on Fridays to clear the local jail out for any new weekend visitors. Contrary to Hollywood's vision of prisoners being moved, the ordeal is quiet and peaceful 99% of the time, and the one percent is a flat tire or car mechanical issue. There hasn't been an escape on a transport in the state of Kentucky since 1971.

The two and half hour trip through the bluegrass of Kentucky isn't guarded with tanks and aircraft either; only two guards make the trip, one drives and the other rides shotgun. Each guard is armed with a handgun, and the windows to the van are tinted so outside observers do not know what or who is inside.

The van is subtlety marked, and tracked with a GPS, but there isn't anyone watching on a computer screen who can shout out, "they stopped moving and are off course!" No, the van is only tracked if it's late. The back of the van is a cell with bars, a door that can only open on the outside, and each prisoner is fitted with leg cuffs which are connected to the handcuffs, and locked into the floor of the van.

There are no stops on this trip which on average takes two hours and twenty nine minutes.

Under protocol, if the van has mechanical issues or a flat tire, the guards will call for local police to come onto the scene. Sometimes the local boys won't even come onto the scene because there isn't a reason, and they don't want to change the tire when the two guards in the van can do it.

When the tire blew out, the van swerved hard to the right, and all the inmates fell forward as the driver regained control and pulled us over. We sat in the blistering cold on the shoulder of the highway just south of Beaver Dam, Kentucky. The wind whipped through the air, slapping up against the van, and we all prayed the guards would leave the heat on while they changed the tire.

As the guards went through an argument of who was going to change the tire, snow began to trickle out of the dirty clouds above us. It wasn't going to accumulate into much more than annoyance, but it was early in the fall for snow.

"It's snowing, so much for the globe warming up, huh, Alice!" The guard riding shotgun joked. They all knew who I was.

"I can change that there tire, boss," inmate Mickey Fint said. Fint was a former mechanic, on his way to the big house for fraud and murder.

"Shut up Fint, everyone knows the last name Fint in Kentucky means fraud," The guard barked back at him. "You probably cannot even change a tire."

"I was a mechanic," Fint responded.

"You're also a Fint!"

"Hush it, Fint, you damn fraud! I better call it in," the other guard said.

A black car with dark tint pulled in behind us, and a matching black SUV with the same mirror tint pulled in front of us.

"Good Samaritans trying to help us," the driver exclaimed.

A man stepped out of the SUV, and walked back towards the van. The guards exited, but another man was coming from behind. Each guard went a different way.

"You boys need help changing the tire?" The man from the car behind us asked. We could hear him clear as day as he was standing right next to the back window.

"Naw, I think we got it."

A local cop pulled in a few seconds later, and a corn-fed young man with an overstuffed jacket stepped out of the cruiser. There were now four men all standing around the flat tire, and the two civilians were adamant that they should help.

"Howdy boys, flat tire, huh?"

"Good afternoon, Officer, I was just telling these two how I got one of those automatic lifts and I can put the van up and help them get back on the road in no time," the man from the car said.

"Yes sir, I am Jim Belcher, and that's my brother, Tim; our daddy was a police officer who served 32 years in New York," the man from the SUV said. "We are driving through on our way to Nashville for a church service at the Grand Ole Opry. We do live sound for all the pastors in our area."

Tim Belcher cut his brother off, "It must be God's plan to have us here with our tire changing equipment."

"It must be," the big local cop nodded. He had no intention of sticking around in the cold and changing a tire. "It is cold as a witches titty out here so if y'all got it handled, I got some paperwork I gotta file back in the office."

"Yes sir, we got this handled," Jim Belcher informed.

"Well, God bless you."

"God bless you, Officer."

"It is cold out here; you care if I sit in the van?" The guard asked Tim and Jim.

"Go right ahead."

The guard opened the door, and turned to the cop walking away, "Take her easy officer, and if she's easy take her twice." After he said it he laughed like a drunk hyena in a cartoon.

"If you need anything else, radio it in."

The wind settled, and the flurries dissipated, but the cold slowly crept into the idle van.

Avery Richards, a 62 year old inmate making his third trip to Eddyville was the first to ask for the heat. "Can you turn on the stinking heat? I can't feel my dick!" He followed up his question by banging his head on the window. Knock. Knock. Knock.

The driver turned around, "Knock it off, Richards!" Then he exited the van to see what was taking so long.

Knock. Knock. Knock. Richard's head was a drumstick, the window his snare. Knock. Knock.

The driver walked right by the window, and banged it with his hand, "Knock it off Richards or I will roll down the freaking windows."

"These windows don't roll down," Richards responded.

Knock. Knock. Knock. Knock. Knock.

Fint turned towards Richards, "Knock it off Avery!"

"Holy shit!" Richards responded.

Jim, who'd been changing the tire, was now holding a pistol pointed right at the two guards. We couldn't hear what was being said though. The driver opened the side door to the van.

"Get inside there, now, move," Jim yelled.

Cars were speeding by us, but they were blind as to what was happening. Both guards piled into the back of the van.

Kevin Noonan, a drunk being sent up for killing a mom and child while drunk driving yelled, "What's going on?"

Both guards sat down next to him, and the driver said, "Shut the fuck up, Noony!"

Noonan didn't stop crying or ask what was happening. Jim slammed the door shut.

The other man, Tim Belcher, opened the door to the van, and pulled out the hidden shotgun, and unloaded it. He also took the pistol from the glove box, placed it into his pants, and then jumped into the driver's seat. Jim opened the passenger door, pointed the gun back at all of us, "Nobody try anything or I will start shooting."

The van took off, and the two cars with black tint pulled out with us. Following the SUV, we went less than a mile and took the first exit off the highway.

"You won't get away with this, this car has GPS tracking," the guard nearest me said.

Jim turned his gun at the guard, "Not another word, or you are dead."

"You're probably going to shoot us anyway!" The other guard said, and I slouched down low in my seat.

Jim pointed the gun at him, and asked, "If you want me to, I can."

The SUV in front of us turned, and the van followed it. There was a sign for an airport, and we were heading towards it. It was the smallest airport in the state. We pulled into the parking lot, followed the SUV through it, and then through a sliding fence. The black car was behind us the whole time.

Pulling onto a small runway, there was a small passenger plane near the end of it. We went straight, and parked next to it.

"Unlock me," Mickey Fint yelled.

Jim jumped out, opened the back door, and to my surprise, he unlocked me.

"Guess you're getting out of here, Moon," Fint said.

"What? Why me?" I begged.

"Let me out too," Avery begged.

"Sure, why not, your old ass ain't going nowhere," Jim turned the key and unlocked him too.

The backdoor opened, and another man looked in at me, "You're coming with us."

"I don't really want to," I answered.

"What?"

"Yeah, I don't really think if I go with you it will be good for me."

Mom's house had been burned down. During my trial, I had to wear a bulletproof vest since there were numerous threats against my life so I wasn't excited about leaving the van with these strangers.

"Alice, if we wanted you dead, we'd have shot you and left. You're coming with us; come on, the plane is ready to depart."

I didn't answer, but Avery did.

"I will go if he won't. I know where the van is going, but I don't know where the plane is going."

"You will sit here until authorities come, but Alice is coming with us."

Avery had a point, I knew where the van was headed. It was headed to the place I would sit for the rest of my life, but we didn't know where the plane was headed.

Exiting the van, my heartbeat was off the scale. Walking with four men and two women, who had come out of the car and SUV, I wasn't as scared as I noticed everyone was just as nervous as me. Tim Belcher stayed in the van, and I turned to watch it drive away.

"Wait, where are they going?"

"To prison, I guess. We will gag up the guards, and tell the staff at Eddyville that they've been trouble, so they might even spend the night in prison until it is all sorted out," A tall man with an accent I couldn't place said. He was dark skinned, and looked latino.

"So where is this plane going?"

"Dominican Republic."

"Why?"

"Why? Because Alice Moon, you have allies, who believe in your mission."

"What mission?" I asked.

"The Owl Rebellion."

"People in the Dominican Republic believe in the Owl Rebellion?"

"People all over the world believe in the Owl Rebellion that you started," A redhead lady said as we walked up the small set of stairs to the plane.

"Really?"

"Yes, really, come on, go take a seat, we need to leave."

Two pilots were in a small cockpit, and they waved at me as I boarded. One was black, and the other latino with a bald shining head. I turned towards the seats of the plane, and Mom was sitting in the second chair in the front row. I ran over to give her a hug.

"Sit down, we gotta leave now," the tall Cuban man told me.

The pilot came over the intercom, "Everyone take a seat and buckle up; it is time to fly. Alice Moon onboard."

"Mom, what's going on?"

"These are your friends; people who supported your message."

"What message?"

"They are all good people, and here for the Owl Rebellion."

"I don't get it, Mom."

"I will explain on the flight."

The plane began to move slowly, and then faster and faster until it was flying, and we were heading southeast into the rising sun. The Owl Rebellion was alive and well.

BOOKS BY THIS AUTHOR

Albert Gum And The Coup D'état To Save Humanity

As climate change wreaks havoc and the water wars end, North America shatters into several new countries in the near-distant future. The eastern coast is a nuclear waste with some rebuilding; the south has reformed around high waters flooding into Georgia: the west is wild, but the old states of Indiana and Michigan areas are running successfully and known as THOD's district.

These areas function with order and are controlled by the self-proclaimed god, THOD. THOD, along with seven senators, including the most beautiful woman in the history of the world, Wren Carter, use propaganda to control the citizens.

Education isn't allowed, and every man, woman, and child must be working. If the hoi polloi is working, they cannot try to overthrow those at the top. Keep the masses dumb and working, feed them propaganda like candy, and keep them fed and entertained when they aren't working.

This bread and circuses routine by THOD and company has worked for over 20 years. The citizens are happy working under the ruse that they are in a socialist society and 'own the means to their production."

Every worker in the district is a millionaire and is trained to be grateful for their work even though money isn't real and most of the jobs are to occupy time only. The dystopian society is called utopian, and the working class believes what they are told.

THOD and his senators live in downtown Indianapolis in the former Circle Center Mall. It is the tallest building left in North America after the water wars, is guarded heavily by military drones and bots, and the seven story building is known as the mall castle.

Albert Gum is a man who doesn't fit into the usual brainwashed crowd. He doesn't love working seven days a week, 50 weeks a year. He doesn't like getting up each morning to work in his pit, and he believes humans should get more than two weeks off in a year. It is dangerous thinking, but his thinking isn't the only danger.

Albert Gum wins a vacation from Wren Carter, but while on his journey to Chicagoland, Albert runs into the father of Beck Lang, outcast senator, and military man, Ryder Lang, and the adventure begins.

Suicide Notes To Kurt Cobain

"Based on true events."

Wanna-be journalist Gunner A. Bush somehow lands his dream job at Rolling Stone magazine. Gunner leaves his hometown of Louisville, Kentucky, to follow in the footsteps of his hero and another Louisvillian, Hunter S. Thompson. Gunner moves to Washington D.C. and hits the campaign trail working for the magazine in the summer of 2016 following both political camps around the country.

As October rolls around, Gunner is yet to be published in the magazine, but he has made deep connections in both political camps. These connections lead him to a rendezvous for an October Surprise. The high-level leak that Gunner lands is the Hollywood Access tape that would make half the world. Gunner is on his way to being published and paid immensely.

Back on the road in St. Louis, covering the Presidential debate in St. Louis, Gunner links up with his best friend from high school, Sawyer Barnes. They party like rockstars, before, during, and after the debates.

Sawyer is going through a divorce and appears to be brainwashed by certain media and planning a mass shooting at his wife's work Halloween party. The details are laid out in his notebook as letters to Kurt Cobain that Gunner accidentally finds and reads.

So Gunner does the only thing he can; he takes Sawyer on the road with him. He wants to keep an eye on him and prevent this from happening. As they drive to Cleveland, Gunner finally realizes his oldest friend isn't the same innocent person he was back in high school. He has become radicalized, and he is adamant that he gets off the road and back to St. Louis before Halloween.

It's a race against time as Gunner tries to figure out how to save his friend from committing an atrocity. Stopping his best friend from committing a mass shooting and suicide isn't his only problem, though, and as the duo returns to Washington D.C, they find the house Gunner has been staying in has been ransacked, fires have been set, and someone left in a hurry. And Gunner's editor at Rolling Stone is dead or missing or worse.